Katherine Beebe

Home Occupations for Little Children

HOME OCCUPATIONS

FOR LITTLE CHILDREN

BY

KATHERINE BEEBE

CHICAGO   NEW YORK

THE WERNER COMPANY

Preface.

In this book the Kindergarten offers to the Home suggestions for the occupation of little children with simple materials. The author does not presuppose a kindergarten training on the part of the mother, nor an ideal environment. She simply takes for granted the child's ceaseless activity and the mother's desire to furnish him with material and opportunity for development.

The occupations here considered are of three kinds. The first are those which require the active participation of an older person; the second, those for which only occasional direction or assistance is necessary; the third, those in which the child can engage by himself. The first two sorts prepare the way for an increase in the number of the third kind of occupations, and all participation and help from the mother ought to be repaid in time by an added power and independence on the part of the child in contriving and carrying on games, plays and childish work by himself. K. B.

Contents.

CHAPTER.   PAGE.

I. "WHAT CAN I DO?" 5

II. STORIES AND MUSIC........................ 17

III. OUT OF DOORS 29

IV. SUGGESTIONS FROM THE KINDERGAR-
TEN GIFTS................................... 46

V. SUGGESTIONS FROM THE KINDERGAR-
TEN OCCUPATIONS......................... 61

VI. WITH NEEDLE AND THREAD 72

VII. WITH PASTE AND SCISSORS............... 82

VIII. WITH PAINTS AND PENCILS.............. 97

IX. CHRISTMAS AND HOLIDAY WORK.......105

X. GAMES AND PLAYS........................118

XI. WORK AND PLAY........................132

LIST OF MATERIALS........................144

Chapter 1.

"WHAT CAN I DO?"

IT is a well-known fact among kindergartners that many children who are restless, turbulent and unruly at home are absolutely happy and good during the morning hours spent in the kindergarten. Some mothers do not understand why this is so, but to the close observer of children its explanation is simple. Children must and will be active. If enough of the right material and opportunity is not supplied them, they will make use of the wrong, to their own and others' disturbance, for they are usually punished or reprimanded for indulging in activities which are unapproved by their elders, in spite of the fact that approved opportunities for activity have not been furnished.

In the (ideal) kindergarten, for three happy hours, the child has a place, a time and an opportunity for a natural growth, during which time he expresses himself freely in play. He has materials with which and playmates with whom to play. He has the sympathy and participation of his elders. He has the help he needs in carrying out his ideas. He is allowed to work in his own way, and he is never heard to say, "What can I do?" As a consequence, he is both happy and good.

Could some such conditions prevail at home during the rest of the day, many a household would be more comfortable, and many a little child transformed from a "troublesome comfort" to a constant delight.

The child wants something to do, and he must have it. Even after the hours which can be spent out of doors are added to those during which he occupies himself with his toys, and to those when he can be directly amused by mother or nurse, and their sum subtracted from the whole number of his waking hours, there still remains that aching void filled too often with the fretful cry, "What can I do?" and a mother's unaccepted suggestions.

"Play with your blocks," she says.

"I don't want to; I don't know anything to make."

"Well, why don't you play with your horses?"

"I don't want to play with my horses!"

"Run down into the kitchen a while and see Maggie."

"I don't want to! There isn't anything to do down there." And so on, the result of such conversations being all too often that he stays with his mother and her guest, either destroying the comfort of both by his restlessness, or sitting quietly listening to conversation which introduces him before his time into the adult world. Surely, anything which will tend to keep him at such times in a child's world of play is worth considering.

Mother and nurse must supply themselves with resources for these hours. There is always a supply of food in the pantry, of clothes in the closets, of remedies in the medicine chest, and of other things necessary to physical comfort and well-being, but there needs to be as well a supply of mental food and stimulus, if the child's mind is to have the power of occupying his hands in a way to keep him normally happy and good. The time is coming when mothers will no more fail to supply the cry of "What can I do?" than they now fail to satisfy that other cry, "Mamma, I am hungry!" The time is coming when a kindergarten training will be a part of every high school, seminary and college course. It is in the hope of placing something in the play-larder that the following chapters are written.

If a child is to play, it goes without saying that he must have a place in which to play; and yet we know that in many houses there is little or no space which he can call his own. Remembering that a child's development, physical, mental and moral, comes to him through play, it seems strange indeed that so little regard is paid to play-space in our domestic and civic economy. Even out of doors the children are not very well provided for, except in the country. In cities and towns the boys are hounded from one place to another by irate property-owners, who do not care where they disport themselves so long as they keep away from their particular premises. They are not even wanted in vacant lots, each set of neighbors driving them away to some other lot. If they play in the streets, pedestrians and drivers are always interfering with games, and people want door-steps and co-pings kept clean.

Indoors it is even worse, for the space available in the average home of the middle class citizen does not permit a special play-room, and the place where play can be carried on freely is usually a small bedroom or part of one, neither of which localities affords scope enough for expanding in-genuity.

It is a pleasure to kindergartners to ob-serve the children's delight in the space, pure and simple, of a good-sized room, and that alone serves to occupy them for con-siderable periods of time, for they can run, jump, throw, dance and do many other things with only themselves and elbow-room for material.

I have no definite suggestions to offer as to play-space in the home. Each mother's problem is a different one, but she who is convinced that her children need play-room as much as they need food or light will manage in some way to secure it for them. There may be mothers who would reduce their number of parlors from two to one; there may be others who, at some personal sacrifice, would build on an extra room; some might sacrifice the order of one particular room, and others might even be driven to the extremity of purchasing folding beds. One mother whom I know surrenders her dining-room, except at meal times. Another has turned the unused barn into a day nursery. The way follows the will, and sacrifices of this sort are generally rewarded a hundred fold.

Servants are often fond of children and willing to help them in their plays, but they are, as a rule, without resource and unable to suggest occupation outside of their own range. Nothing is better for children than a participation in the work of the house, and nothing is more delightful to them in their earliest years. Happy is the mother who has a cook, housemaid or other servant to whom she can explain the necessity of allowing the children to "help," and who will, with some degree of intelligence, follow her suggestions.

Many a servant has both time and inclination to be of real service to the children of the house, if she but knew how to do it. If the mother's head be enlisted in the cause as well as her heart, she can make good use of this friendly feeling by furnishing a little stimulus and material when it is impossible for her to give her own time to her little ones.

The companionship of servants, while it may be disastrous and sometimes is pernicious, is not altogether the evil some would have us think. Too much of it would, of course, subject a child, during the plastic period, to influences which any mother would deplore; but, like all other forces, when handled and used judiciously, it may have its good uses. Servants are oftentimes more near to the child's state of mind than his adult relatives. They are frequently only grown-up children, and really enjoy child-like employments. Irish girls are born child-lovers and sympathizers. The Swedes, while less demonstrative, are usually honest and trustworthy. To share the work of these friendly members of the household, and to share with them their own little interests, is usually a part of every child's life where there are servants in the family; and so, if from the play-larder the mother can give to those servants into whose hands the children must fall occasionally some material or suggestions, both servant and child will not only be made more comfortable, but many an evil hour will be kept from taking a place in the time-chain of the child's existence.

Children, to be truly happy, must have the companionship of other children. Most parents, believing this, allow their children friends and playmates; but there are mothers who, in their desire to keep the child's mind uncontaminated, deprive him of this necessary stimulus. Students of child-nature are beginning to think that there is less danger from chance companionships than has been imagined, presupposing a sound home training. Just as a sound body resists exposure and contagion, and throws off disease which is the undoing of a weaker one, so a sound mind and healthy soul will resist evil. Unless a child's companions are known to be really objectionable, the evil of no companionship is apt to be greater than the risk run in letting him play with his mates.

Other mothers there are who, in their devoted absorption in their children, forget or ignore this need of child-life. That their own companionship is not enough does not occur to them. Such mothers should at least try the experiment of allowing their children to play with others of the same age before coming to the conclusion that playmates are unnecessary.

Our country is full not only of children who are suffering for companionship; it is also full of respectable, hard-working families who have so many children that but few advantages and little attention can be given them. Some sort of social exchange, with schools and kindergartens for centers, seems a possibility of the future in the consideration of these problems.

It has been stated that there are 350,000 homeless children in the United States, but happily we hear every little while of one family and another who has taken one of these little ones in, either to brighten a childless home or to bring companionship to a lonely little only child. In this latter case, it is hard to say which child is the more benefited.

Many articles have been written by kindergartners of more or less experience, with the alluring title of ''The Kindergarten in the Home,'' which have proved disappointing to the reader. The writer either presupposes a kindergarten training on the part of the mother which does not exist, or the directions are too elaborate to be easily followed. Often the ideas suggested, when carried out, yield but scant results, the work occupying the average child about ten minutes, more or less, at the end of which period both mother and child are about where they were before. I recall one such article, which, when boiled down, conveyed to the mother the two ideas that the kindergarten balls should be introduced into the nursery, and that with a four-inch square of folding paper many beautiful forms could be made.

More than this is necessary. The kindergarten has much to offer to the home in the way of helpful suggestions, and it can do this without asking the mother to do at home the same things that are done in the kindergarten by trained teachers. Often materials which can be used and work which can be done in the kindergarten are impracticable in the home, and *vice versa*. The home needs the kindergarten to lead the way and provide stimulus to developing action. The kindergarten needs the home to complete, carry out and extend work which can be only begun in the limited time at the kindergartner's disposal. The principles of Froebel can be applied to the chairs, pans, spools, buttons and strings with which the child occupies himself at home, and it can also impart a new life and suggestiveness to toys, pets and all home materials.

Chapter II.

STORIES AND MUSIC.

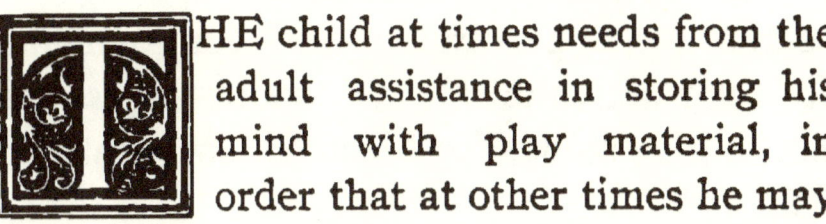HE child at times needs from the adult assistance in storing his mind with play material, in order that at other times he may have a stock of ideas from which to draw. His imagination needs food and stimulus other than that supplied by the ordinary happenings of his daily life. This is proven in the kindergarten by the difference in the power to play existing between children who come from homes where this stimulus is supplied, and those who come from homes where it is lacking. The more fortunate little ones are seldom at a loss for play material, while the others often have actually to be taught to play those games in which thought and imagination play a part.

Children of this first class, as we all know, love to dramatize the life about them, are fond of games which are largely, if not wholly, of a physical nature, and will indulge both of these tendencies freely, but while in spite of this they continue to demand "something to do," we who have charge of them will have to continue our search for opportunities and employments for their active minds and bodies if we are not to give stones for bread and serpents for fish.

In the homes of the poor, for obvious reasons, the children seldom have stories told to them, rarely if ever hear story books read, and never have music adapted to their minds and hearts provided for them. Consequently the beautiful imagery of song and story is lost to them. Their imaginations are starved and their souls often remain unawakened long past the time for such unfolding, while many powers never develop at all which exist potentially in them. It is true that poets and artists sometimes come from very humble walks of life, but in most cases Genius or Nature provided the necessary stimulus. Happily the schools of to-day are doing for the less fortunate what is done for the more fortunate at home.

It is with the children of the ordinary well-to-do class that we have now to deal, however, and we know that these children love stories told and read, and that their souls open to music. These things are such potent factors in, and such a vital part of kindergarten life, that they surely belong in the child's home-life as well. Kindergartners never have time enough with their children to give them half the songs and stories which they really want to give, and they would be glad to pass over to the home their uncompleted work and store of material to help fill those hours which echo with the cry, "What can I do *now?*" In the kindergarten the stories are not told and then dismissed as something finished and gotten through with. They are carefully selected in the first place, and there is a pedagogical reason for each selection with which just now we have nothing to do. One prime object is to feed the growing imagination and stock it with play material, as well as, in technical phrase, to help the child to self-expression. The stories told are not only retold by the children later on, but they are also "worked out;" that is, the children picture the story, or such part of it as appeals to them, on the blackboard or with paper and pencil. They also play it with their blocks and sticks; they model objects suggested by it with clay; they cut these objects from paper, sew them or paint them, as the exigency of the occasion demands.

Children love the definite, and gladly take and work out definite suggestions. When clay, paint, paper, or other material is put into a child's hands and he is told to play with it, an active imagination will sometimes supply a sufficiency of ideas to be expressed, but usually he soon reaches his limitations, if not on the first occasion then very soon after, and will be apt to say, "I don't know what to make."

"Oh, make a horse!" mother or nurse will suggest.

"I don't want to make a horse," says the child, in whose mind only images of indefinite and general horses are called up by the word. But, if after hearing Longfellow's beautiful story of "The Bell of Atri," that particular horse is suggested, it becomes another matter, and one object often suggests another, until the whole story is worked out by busy fingers stimulated by a live imagination.

The mother then wants from the kindergartner a list of stories to be told and of books to be read which shall fill her child's mind with beautiful images which can be expressed by the little hands so anxious to *do*. She should adopt in the nursery the kindergarten method of working out or making these stories with whatever material is at hand. These home stories should not only fill the time in which they are read or told, but many happy after hours; often only a suggestion will be necessary to set the children to work, and sympathy and appreciation only will keep them at it.

With some children the mother may find it necessary to participate actively in the play to show the children how it may be done, and to get them started; but this she will not accomplish by playing *for* them, but by playing *with* them, and encouraging their efforts by judicious praise and admiration.

Stories are dramatized in the kindergarten with great success, and children who can be led to do this at home will have an inexhaustible store of material for play hours. I know of one group of ten-year-old children who played "The Prince and the Pauper" a whole winter, and of another who played "Robinson Crusoe" day in and day out. One little home kindergarten went to Greenland one snowy day and lived there for three weeks.

If the mother's own imagination will seize upon those particular stories which are best adapted to dramatic action, if she will aid the children a little in their representations, occasionally take part, and always sympathize, she will soon develop a dramatic talent, which, to say the least, will make stormy days interesting in her household.

As a rule it is hardly wise for the mother and kindergartner to be using the same ma-

terial in the same way. Fortunately this is
rarely done, as only a trained kindergartner
has the power of using the material without
wearying the child or reaching his limitations too soon. Mothers are often made to
feel that the knowledge they lack and should
possess is the knowledge which kindergartners use in giving gift and occupation lessons.
Not that this knowledge would not be of
great advantage to any mother, but the point
is that there is much that she can do without
it. Such a profound knowledge of the possibilities of the gifts and occupations as
would enable her to continue, enlarge and
supplement the kindergartner's work would
be of the greatest use, but to be able to give
the child the same work with blocks or
sticks which he has had or will have in the
kindergarten is of no particular advantage,
except when the child cannot go to the kindergarten.

In the matter of stories, however, she need
have no fears of trenching on kindergarten
ground. When a child loves a story he
will hear it many times, and one often-told

and well-loved tale is frequently better than many.

One direct help which the kindergartner craves of the mother is her encouragement to the child to retell at home the stories he has heard in the kindergarten. If in addition to this he will at home play or work out these stories the kindergartner's work will be carried on.

Some stories are better told than read, others make good reading, and it is important that a child should learn early to listen to reading. For children under three years old there are no better books than the bound volumes of "Babyland;" "The Baby World," compiled from St. Nicholas; "Mother Goose;" and the "Finger Plays," by Emilie Poulsson. For the four-year-olds get the bound and current volumes of "Child Garden;" and "In the Child's World," by Emilie Poulsson. For the children of five and six there are "The Story Hour," by Kate Douglas Wiggin; "In Storyland," by Elizabeth Harrison; the new editions of Grimm and Andersen, Bible Stories, Greek and Norse myths; Æsop's Fables; tales from Roman and American History; Jane Andrews' books; "Seaside and Wayside," by Julia McNair Wright; "Adventures of a Brownie," by Miss Mulock; some of Miss Alcott's stories for little children, and such poems for children as Eliot, Childs, Whittier, Stevenson and Field have written or selected for us. Susan Coolidge has written some very good tales for young children, and there are, of course, many others which time and space forbid me to mention. Some classic stories which are excellent for telling are "Rip Van Winkle," "The Pied Piper," "The Bell of Atri," "Paul Revere," and "Rhoecus." If to this list is added bound and current volumes of "St. Nicholas," "Six-year-old" will have a very fair library.

Much of what has been said of stories applies also to music. In the kindergarten the songs are dramatized and often worked out with different kinds of material. If at home the child sings for his mother and other members of the household, if he is aided in the correct use of words and tones, the kindergartner's work is continued. It often happens that in teaching a song little brains do not always get the ideas which the words of the song and the teacher's explanations are designed to convey. In the necessary concert teaching many a small mistake escapes the ear of the kindergartner which the mother can correct. For instance, one little girl sang for the words "All for the little ones' Christmas joys," "All for the little ones' Christmas *George*," and the teacher was greatly obliged to the mother for detecting and correcting a mistake which probably would have escaped her entirely.

In all homes, whether the children attend a kindergarten or not, the beautiful song books of these latter days should be in use. Mother and children should sing together, the children should be taught to sing for others, and where it is possible the song-story should be acted out in a play spirit. These song books furnish music for almost every occasion in child-life, and songs learned by the children can be *used* in a way that will make life happier for all who hear them. No kindergartner needs to say that she disapproves unqualifiedly of showing children off. Mothers still do this to their own and the children's undoing, and the songs and plays of the kindergarten seem to furnish added temptation to these fond and foolish parents to go on with the process of brushing off the bloom of childish unconsciousness. But children can sing for others without being shown off. Christmas, Thanksgiving and Easter songs can be sung on the occasions for father. Groups of neighborhood children can give little serenades and concerts to friends and neighbors judicious enough to listen respectfully and comment sensibly. What invalid or convalescent would not rejoice to hear songs sung by happy children's voices? What family festival would not be sweeter for the childish songs which voice the soul of the occasion?

There are a few homes where the mother or father, or both, can and will take the time to sing with the children, to teach them the beautiful songs which are so **many** that the teacher can only use a fraction of them, to learn the songs which they sing in school or kindergarten, and so to have in their home music for the children as well as for themselves.

Among the approved present day music books for children are those prepared by Eleanor Smith, one by Mildred and Patty Hill, the Reinike Collection, Tomlins' "Child Garden of Song" and other books, and the St. Nicholas songs.

With any or all of these books many a happy evening hour can be passed and many a profitable Sunday afternoon, for the devotional songs in these collections are *good music*, which is more than can be said of most Sunday school melodies. With their aid and the mother's, the house may become musical with child-like songs, and delightful surprises and joyous occasions provided for. Mental and spiritual food for growing minds and souls can be given in this way, and the store of play material enhanced as well.

Chapter III.

OUT OF DOORS.

THE Nature Study of schools and kindergartens is full of suggestiveness for the home occupation of little children in their outdoor hours and vacation days. The province of the kindergarten in the matter of Science teaching, and also of the nursery, is chiefly to inspire a love of nature and her works in the children, although by so doing the observation is quickened and all the faculties aroused. All analysis and classifying should come later.

It is a mistake to think that little children unaided will become observers and lovers of Nature. We of the present generation have but to look back to our own childhood to prove that. In spite of a child's love of out-door life and his keen interest in all he sees, that interest will become dulled and blunted if his questions are not answered and his efforts appreciated. His very love for out doors may become a purely physical feeling, and he can soon become both blind and deaf to Nature's teachings. On the other hand it is very easy to lead a little child from his Heaven-sent beginning in Nature Study into a real love for and intelligent interest in all natural phenomena. The chief necessaries for this are appreciation of and sympathy with his efforts, to which must be added opportunity for further observation. To be much out of doors with the children, to follow their restless leadings, to be interested where they are interested, and to be able to lead them into "other fields and pastures new" when they are ready to go, is to "live with our children" as Froebel hoped we should some day.

This lover of children laid great stress on sense games in his book for mothers. He would have them train the senses of their children to acuteness and discrimination by means of play. In one kindergarten this idea was carried out last September by means of the fruits so abundant at that time.

A number of these were provided, the number suited to the ages and abilities of the children, who named them and counted them, and also drew them with colored chalk. One child's eyes being blindfolded, another child hid one of the fruits. It was then the turn of the blinded one to guess which fruit was missing, and if he guessed correctly he was "heartily cheered;" if his guess was wrong, he tried again another time. This was played as long as the children were interested, and on another occasion a game of guessing feeling the fruits, filled a half hour, while still later they were guessed by smelling and tasting. Such games as these, when taught to children and played occasionally with them, ought to set them going in this particular direction to their own physical, mental and spiritual upbuilding. Older children delight in these simple kindergarten games and seldom have the opportunity they wish to learn and use them. In their playing school or playing kindergarten they could amuse both themselves and younger brothers and sisters in this way, for the games can be played with nuts, leaves, shells, stones, blocks, flowers, grains, children, and miscellaneous objects.

Nuts make delightful playthings used after this manner, and kindergarten children delight in playing they are squirrels and hunting the nuts previously hidden by one of their number, especially if privileged to eat the nuts at the end of the game. Hunting nuts in the real woods is a psychological basis for this play as well as a joy which children should taste oftener than they usually do, for in these days of railroads and electric cars the woods are not so very far off, and once a year at least there should be a nutting party in every well-regulated family.

If in the Indian Summer days, after the leaves are off the trees and the birds have flown, a collection of nests could be made from the woods, parks or suburbs, by means of excursions in company with a boy of tree-climbing age and propensities, a work worth doing would be wrought in the minds and hearts of all concerned.

Nothing gives children more pleasure in the Fall than milkweed pods full of the "dainty milkweed babies." Go where these are to be found in September or October; bring them home and let them dry in the house; explain to the children why they are furnished with wings and how the wind plants them; let them have some pods to play with out of doors on windy days; and let them make pretty winter bouquets of dry clusters of the pods for friends and relatives. Little girls can make down pillows of the seeds for their dolls, and an ambitious child could even collect enough for a down pillow for a real baby. Thistle down can also be used in this way.

During the autumn the different kinds of seeds and seed-pods greatly interest the children, who would enjoy gathering them if there was any reason which appealed to them for so doing. The interest of the older people in such a collection is sufficient oftentimes to stimulate them to effort, but a real object, such as saving for next year's garden, making a collection for a present to somebody, or gathering quantities to be sent to city relations, city kindergartens or anyone poor or sick, appeals more to the child. He is a reasonable little being and does not care to do things which are not "worth while," much more than we do. An examination of the seeds with a microscope will repay anyone, and no child will fail to be interested in the perfectly formed leaves tucked up in many seeds all ready for next year.

When the leaves begin to fall, playthings are literally showered on those children whose eyes and hearts true sympathy has opened. It is a commonly pathetic sight in autumn days to see a little child gathering the bright leaves with a wistful what-can-I-do-with-you expression, only to throw them away. If he brings them into the house, they are often unnoticed and uncared for, and the most he can expect is to have them put into a glass of water and forgotten. Kindergarten children bring leaves to their teachers by the bushel and the wise use made of them in the child-garden can also be made of them at home. The names can be learned; guessing games can be played with them; they can be traced, drawn and painted; beautiful borders and patterns can be laid with them; tea-tables can be decorated with them; wreaths and festoons can transform the child into an autumn picture for his father; they can also be pressed, varnished and waxed. In our kindergarten the waxed leaves of last October decorate our tables during the rest of the year for birthday or other parties.

In the great masses of dead rustling leaves are delightful places to play squirrel and rabbit games, and for a romp, what material is better adapted for tossing, rolling and throwing? Children will rake leaves patiently, if, when father comes home, they can be present at the bonfire, and to go to the woods with older friends and bring home great bouquets of red and yellow to make the house beautiful is a long remembered joy.

Baskets of acorns will be gladly gathered if they can be used, and in many a city kindergarten they would be treasures indeed. The double acorn cups can be strung by slipping the string between the two cups. These productions give much pleasure to the children who have to find the double acorns and string them, as well as to the baby-brother, sister or neighbor to whom they can be presented.

Corn-cobs in quantity made in olden times, and still make, charming playthings, and a corn-husk dolly would be a greater treasure than one from a store to many an indulged child. Wild cucumbers and tooth-picks will stock a minature farm with bristling pigs, and the vines can be grown in almost any spot of earth where there is good soil. Stones always interest children, but the interest is a fleeting one for the reason that limitations are reached so soon. If a place is prepared for a collection of the most attractive stones, and if the mother can tell her child a little of their history, an added stimulus to patient hunting and sorting is given. Duplicate collections can be made for friends and sick children, and bottles containing a little water filled with bright colored pebbles make a gift for a convalescent which will afford him a little, and the giver much pleasure.

The bright berries of autumn, the haws, thorn-apples, and cranberries are beautiful for stringing purposes, making a pleasant change from beads and buttons. In season, clover heads, dandelion heads and the tiny flowers which make up the lilac's blossom make good material for stringing, and this industry should be added to the familiar occupations of making dandelion curls and chains.

Get a sheet of dark bronze paper on whose white side flying birds can be traced from a pattern. The model can be drawn and cut out of pasteboard, or a picture be made to serve the purpose. Let the children trace and cut out a flock of these birds; fasten them high up on the nursery wall headed south in the fall, and make others which can head north in the spring. Sets of these can be made for friends and saved for Christmas and birthday gifts; for a present which is not the child's own has little value, as a gift, in his eyes compared with one which has cost him effort or sacrifice.

Where children can have the use of hammers and nails they can make crude bird houses in which real birds will live all summer, and they will often spend a half-hour raveling out bits of coarsely woven cloth, which, hung on bushes, trees or fences in the spring, are to furnish the birds with nest-building material.

A globe, or other receptacle, in which fish can be kept will be a treasure to children old enough to go about alone or fortunate enough to possess a grown-up real friend who will take them occasionally where they want to go. It will give a reason for the collection of frog's eggs, tadpoles, tiny minnows, crawfish and mussels. How children love these things, and how seldom is it worth their while to bring them home we both know and remember! "They are very interesting, dear," says mamma, trying to repress a look of disgust, "but we have no place to keep such things. Throw them away.'' A tub in which water from their own homes and breeding places can be placed seems to agree best with tadpoles, by the way.

To learn the trees by name, to know their blossoms and seed is a pursuit in which old and young may join with mutual pleasure and profit. The country is full of thriving little seedling trees which, striving for life in vacant lots, parkways and roadsides, would one day become real trees, if transplanted into an amateur nursery. Some one once suggested that, if for every child born, a tree, seedling, or seed were planted the forestry problem would be solved.

A miniature fruit farm can be made by planting apple, peach, plum, pear, cherry, orange or lemon seeds, and, while it may never reach a very advanced state, the planting of the seeds, the watching for the first shoots, and the observation of the tiny trees will fill up some of those industrial vacancies for which we are trying to provide. When we were children there were few springs when we did not plant a vegetable garden in an old dish-pan or cheese-box, using for planting purposes one potato, one beet, one onion, one turnip, and one anything else we could get.   I do not remember that there was ever any outcome to this agricultural enterprise, but I have a very distinct recollection of the pleasure this tilling of the soil gave to me.   I will add that we lived in a city and that our backyard was boarded over, but to the true farmer-spirit all things are possible.

The collecting of cocoons in the fall will give occupation at that time as well as later on when the moths come out.   These are found in both city and country, and a study of them will prove most interesting.

Of the small snail shells found on the lake shore, and in gravel piles, strings can be made, as they usually have holes in them. A child will hunt patiently for these treasures even when he has not the hope of using them.   Babies and younger children are delighted recipients of such gifts as these, and the fact that they so soon tire of them need not affect either the work or the satisfaction of the donor.

Drinking cups can be made of large leaves pinned together by their stems, and those of us who read the Rollo books long ago remember that the backs of the lilac leaves can be used for slates if pins are the pencils. I have known kindergarten graduates to reproduce their brief educational experience, using pebbles, twigs, leaves, dandelion stems and burrs for material. The pebbles were seeds, the twigs sticks, the leaves folding papers, and the burrs clay. They even wove coarse grass into mats and did pricking with thin leaves and stiff grasses. The burdock's prickly seed-pod can be made, not only into baskets and nests, but into animals, furniture and almost any sort of object. It is well to protect little hands with old gloves for this work, for the burrs leave invisible splinters in the fingers, which are very uncomfortable. Until one has tried it one does not know how lifelike and satisfactory to the children are the squirrels, rabbits, dogs, cats and elephants which can be made of either the green or the brown burrs. The golden rod galls can, with a knife and the addition of grasses or stems, be transformed into tiny vases and dishes. Flower dolls make beautiful fairies with their pansy, daisy or dandelion faces, their leaf shawls and poppy or morning glory skirts, and "pea-pod boats with rose-leaf sails" are delightful possibilites.

I know one child whose delight it was to make fairy-lands, filling a shady corner or shallow box with moss-covered earth in which she planted miniature trees, flowers and shrubs, sinking a saucer, which could be filled with water, into the ground for a lake.

On the lake or seashore the construction of geographical formations, hills, mountains, islands and rivers, gives even a little child at times more satisfaction than his own rather aimless building of houses. One group of children last summer made the Michigan fruit farms and a smaller Lake Michigan, over whose waters fruit-laden boats sailed to city markets.

Radical as it sounds water makes a delightful plaything, but it is seldom used because—it is too much trouble! Happy is the child equipped for play in a fresh puddle left by the rain, or in a tub of water in the back yard! Happy is the child who is sometimes dressed for a frolic in a warm summer shower, who on hot days is allowed to play in the bath-tub or with the hose! Happy are those children who, when taken to shore or beach, are dressed, or undressed, so that they will not have to be cautioned every other minute not to get wet! The old familiar rhyme beginning "Mother, may I go out to swim?"—you know the rest —would be appreciated by many children on lake shore and ocean beach if they happened to know it.

Mother Nature with her sunshine, rain, wind, hail, snow and various commotions and combinations of the elements is always ready to play with the children, and they with her, were they only allowed to do so. They are not allowed because of the fear that they will soil or injure their clothes, hurt themselves, take cold, or be too much trouble to some one, and so they lose many hours which, through the happiest play, might bring to them health, courage, freedom and joy.

The catnip by the roadsides can be gathered into bunches and dried for Christmas gifts to all the owners of pussy-cats in the family connection. Gifts of freshly gathered chickweed and plantain seeds will be appreciated by bird owners, who too often forget or neglect to procure these delicacies for their pets.

Little house gardens can be made in boxes of earth, sponges or cotton. Sweet potato vines can be grown in a wide-mouthed jar or bottle filled with water, and all of these simple things bring pleasure and profit to the children if only "somebody cares." The little folks will be glad to be taken into partnership with the mother who cultivates house plants.

The real out-door garden should be a part of every child's life, but here again "too much trouble" deprives children of a heaven-sent pleasure and means of development. To help a child plant a garden and teach him to take care of it *is* a task, such a task as it is worth while to attend to as one would attend to the making of beds or dusting of furniture. When once we take hold of a thing and make a regular business of it, it ceases to be a care and an annoyance. This rule holds good in regard to many of the things which we ought to do with and for our children, things which we leave to chance or do not do at all.

To bring flowers of his own raising into the family life or to take them to friends, invalids, hospital or city, is a spiritual experience of which children should not be deprived. Give them a chance to ''continue in well-doing'' and to exercise unselfishness.

It is useless to start a child's garden and expect him to take care of it alone and of his own accord. He needs to be lead by sympathy and participation to the joys of fruition for many seasons, in order that in time he may become a true nature-lover and gardener.

Chapter IV.

SUGGESTIONS FROM THE KINDER-GARTEN GIFTS.

MOTHERS are usually urged by kindergartners and others to get the Hailman Beads for home use, but the possibilities of this gift are soon exhausted if one does not know a little about it. These beads are much used in the kindergarten and perhaps if a child attends one regularly he will get as much of this particular play there as he needs. For children who cannot go to a kindergarten there is no better plaything, and little folks of three and four years of age will spend many a quiet hour by mother's side with them, needing very little actual help beyond a few directions and the ever-necessary sympathy.

These beads are small one-half inch spheres, cubes and cylinders, both colored and uncolored. For form-work the latter are the better, and both kinds can be bought by the box or in bulk. I have never yet seen a kindergarten which had a sufficient quantity of them, and I have never yet seen a lay purchaser who did not consider one box an ample quantity, and who did not wonder later on why the baby cared so little about stringing them.

I would advise the purchase of this gift in bulk, one lot of uncolored, and another lot of colored beads, and more of the latter than the former. Instead of giving them at once to the child for desultory, haphazard and general play, they should be put away and for some time only brought out when a definite work or play can be instigated and guided. If this is done the beads will long remain a thing to be desired, and by means of this definiteness of purpose on the part of the mother, the time will come, when, if they are put into a child's hands and he is told to play with them, he will be able to amuse himself in any one of the delightful ways which he has been taught, and he will also invent new combinations of form and number.

For convenience I mark off this work into lessons or steps.

1. From uncolored beads, string all spheres.
2. "   "   "   "   " cubes.
3. "   "   "   "   " cylinders.
4. "   colored   "   "   " red beads.
5. "   "   "   "   " blue "
6. "   "   "   "   " yellow "
7. "   "   "   "   " orange "
8. "   "   "   "   " green "
9. "   "   "   "   " purple "
10. Number lessons in uncolored beads as: One sphere, one cube, one cylinder.
11. Two spheres, two cubes, two cylinders, etc.
12. String colored beads in the order of the spectrum.
13. Number lessons *ad infinitum* in combinations of the colored beads.
14. Invent combinations in uncolored beads.
15. "   "   " colored   "

For stringing purposes nothing is better than strong shoestrings. When a string of beads is finished, or a lesson completed, it may be worn as a decoration, but must be saved until evening to be shown and explained to papa. After a definite lesson of this sort is completed in the kindergarten the children are allowed to do as they please with a quantity of the material for a while. Some do the work of the lesson over again, some invent new combinations, some string the beads in no apparent order but with great apparent pleasure. That free play should follow definite work with almost all material is a safe rule for the nursery as well as the kindergarten. In this particular case if the free-play string shows any sort of order or definiteness it too should be saved until evening and papa informed that somebody's busy fingers did that one all alone.

With burnt matches companies of gay soldiers can be made with these beads by running the match through the holes in a cube, cylinder and sphere successively, and standing the result upright on the cube end. Splendid processions can be formed, and if the companies are arranged in colors the result is very pleasing. These same soldiers, if transformed by the imagination into school or kindergarten children, will make good playthings, as with blocks the schoolhouse can be built and a whole educational scheme dramatized. I have seen kindergarten pupils place these bead children on a circle and go through their whole list of games, songs and marches with them. If the real kindergarten, the real school or the real home is represented, certain bead structures representing certain real persons, the play becomes even more delightful to the children.

On longer sticks the beads become logs, beams and other objects, and they can also be made to reproduce in miniature the forms made with the larger blocks. A farm, a house, a water-wheel and mill, or in fact any desired set of objects, can be constructed with these little playthings. If when giving them in this way the mother is wise enough to seize on the set of circumstances most prominent in the child's mind, a recent visit, a prospective excursion, the big department store, or the coming Thanksgiving celebration, she will discover new possibilities both in her child and the material.

One other game with these beads which was played successfully in a kindergarten may be suggestive of other similar ones. The red spheres were sorted out and transformed into strawberries, for it was June. The room became a meadow and after one child had hidden the beads the others took their baskets and went strawberrying, having a supper afterwards of the berries brought home. This pretending play—pretending to set the table, eat, drink and clear away, or do anything else of the sort, has an unfailing charm at any time if entered into by mother or teacher with any sort of dramatic zest. Nothing will sooner bring soul into a child's eyes and sunshine into his face. If you doubt this try it and see, not forgetting the zest.

Old fashioned glass beads make good presents for small convalescents and good playthings at any time, if kept out of sight and produced only on occasion.

If old visiting cards are cut into exact squares and triangles the children will be glad to amuse themselves laying forms with

them. They should be cut on a two-inch
scale and it will be well to limit the quantity
used at times, taxing the ingenuity of the
child by stimulating him to do what he can
with four, six, eight or twelve cards. Side-
walks, streets, car-tracks, enclosed spaces,
steps and borders can be laid on the nursery
floor; chairs, tables, houses, barns, castles
and stars can be represented, and best of all,
beauty forms and geometrical designs will
suggest themselves, or can be copied from
patterns in wall paper, carpets, oil-cloths and
other articles. Give the squares first and
lead the child to do what he can with them,
then add the different triangles, the right
isosceles, equilateral, obtuse isosceles, and
right scalene in turn, and finally let combinations be made of two or more forms. Any
of the forms or figures laid can be easily
copied on paper or blackboard, and both
tablets and the drawings of them can be
colored. When the forms are to be drawn
it would be well if the child had a good
blank book in which to preserve his efforts,
for the same amount of care will not be put

on a slip of paper which will probably be thrown away, as on the leaf of the drawing book which is to be kept always, and which can be shown to papa any night when a new picture is added.

In giving the child this plaything, help him from his indefinite to definite action and work.

A few cedar blocks, such as are used in paving streets, split up into sticks about eight inches long and half an inch thick, will furnish a new plaything. Pine sticks will do of course, but the cedar block lends itself so readily to this kind of division and is so fragrant that it is to be preferred. The bulk of this material, for the sticks should fill a good-sized basket, pleases the child; for psychologists tell us that the large muscles develop first, and that large playthings best meet nature's demands in the early years. With these sticks the children can, in a crude way, outline forms and make pictures which express their thoughts. Here again streets and railroad tracks suggest themselves. The simple mathematical forms, squares, oblongs, triangles, trapeziums, trapezoids, pentagons, hexagons, octagons and the like give a pleasure to children which must be experienced to be realized. They are so easily changed into life and beauty forms by the addition of other sticks, and are so readily converted by repetition into border patterns, that their possibilities seem almost endless. Simple houses of the old corn-cob style can be built, the zigzag Virginian rail fence can be exactly reproduced, and many other forms outlined or copied. Among these are houses, bird-houses, churches, fences, ladders, doors, windows, furniture, clocks, stars, wheels, boats, cars, and almost any other desired objects. The thoughts filling the child's mind, whether they be of the coming Christmas, the new baby or the home kitchen, can be expressed with this material, and a child will play in this quiet way a long time making something for mamma to guess.

" Oh, go play with your sticks ! " may not always bring about the desired result, but, " Oh, Helen, let us make the big

Thanksgiving table at grandma's!'' will probably accomplish something. If you add, '' Can you make chairs for them all? Make the church where grandpa goes! Now try the stove where they will cook the turkey! Make what you want for Christmas and see if I can guess what you make.'' In all probability Helen will be happily occupied for a long time, especially if she copies into her drawing book the forms she has laid.

These large sticks keep their places so well when laid, and so adapt themselves to the floor where children play so much, that they have peculiar advantages for a child's first attempt at sticklaying. Later the slats, splints and kindergarten sticks may replace them.

Outlining with seeds of different sorts will give pleasure to many children under right conditions, these conditions being sometimes participation, at all times sympathy, and the necessary thought stimulus; that is, that the work be the expression of thought that interests. Groups of objects or single forms carefully laid and preserved for someone's

pleasure, will keep restless fingers busy on
many a rainy afternoon, and the collecting
and sorting of various seeds, such as apple
seeds, melon seeds, sunflower seeds, corn,
beans, lentils and coffee, is a part of the
work. A seed box can be set up in the Fall,
or at any other time of the year, into which
seeds can be dropped against the rainy days
when the accumulation can be sorted and
used.

With blocks, as with seeds and sticks, to
suggest representations of those objects or
subjects which at the time are most engag-
ing the child's attention, is often to oil the
mainspring of action. It must be borne in
mind constantly while reading these directions that all the times when a child will
happily and rightfully employ himself are
clear gain, and these suggestions are to be
used chiefly when his resources are exhausted.

Of course with their blocks children will
play by themselves for long periods of time,
but when the time comes when they say,
" We don't know what to build," it is well

to have a few ideas to offer, as for instance, a suggestion to build a big barn with a large door, at the farther end of the room, and roll balls, which for the time being become horses or cows, into it. Strongly built bird-houses into which bits of paper rolled into balls for flying birds can be thrown, high towers against which balls can be rolled, are all practicabilities. The tower game is a sort of nursery ninepins, and the one who succeeds in overturning the structure has the privilege of inventing a new one. A telephone game with blocks for poles and strings for wires is another suggestion. A farm enclosed with blocks, elaborated with other materials and toys, and kept for the friends who are to be invited in to see it; churches, castles, boats and factories; models of the houses in which real people live; foundations laid as real foundations are with gum tragacanth paste for mortar, and stories and experiences worked out are among the many things which can be done with blocks. If, for instance, the Three Bears is the last tale heard or the one most prominent in the child's mind, the blocks can be made to tell the story over again to papa or some one else. The little house, the three beds, the three chairs, the bowls, stove and table, can be built and placed in a safe spot. Such careful preservation of work will go a long way toward correcting destructive tendencies. Indeed it is not to be wondered at that children are careless and destructive when we reflect how often a whole afternoon's effort is left in fragments on the floor, consigned to the flames or buried in the waste basket.

For nursery use kindergartners recommend cubical blocks two inches square, some of which should be divided into triangular prisms. Oblong blocks 4x2x1 should form another set. The use of these need not preclude the use of others already in possession, for any or all of these suggestions can be carried out with whatever blocks are on hand, but if one is buying new blocks, and can have this particular kind made by a carpenter, the child himself can have the pleasure of pasting pictures on them, which will be infinitely better than buying for him those blocks which already have pictures on their several sides; and if he does not care to do this pasting there is no harm done, as the plain wooden blocks yield the most satisfactory architectural results anyway.

For the yard, warm basement, or attic there can be no better plaything than a load or part of a load of cedar paving blocks. With these all sorts of houses, stores, boats and forts, large enough to get into bodily, can be built. Schools, churches, kindergartens and railroad trains can be furnished with them, and a thousand other uses such as would never occur to the adult mind will be discovered for these fascinatingly big cylinders. No one who has watched the children on a street which was being paved with these blocks will doubt this. The objection urged to such a plaything as this will doubtless be that the children would play with them delightedly for a little while and then tire of them. This is true of not only cedar blocks, but of many other toys, such as bicycles, wagons, rocking horses and even ponies. It is not child nature to concentrate very long on any one thing, however much it delights at first. We overlook this fact when it touches the inexpensive dolls, tin dishes, jumping frogs, and the like, but notice it at once when the Bagatelle Board is deserted for the popgun, and the big Baby House left desolate because of a new jumping rope. But just as surely as a child's natural fickleness leads him to desert one plaything for another, just so surely will it lead him back to it again and again, and the more adjustable, transformable and capable of change a plaything is the oftener will childish affections revisit it.

Chapter V.

SUGGESTIONS FROM THE KINDER-GARTEN OCCUPATIONS.

THE weaving of paper mats is a favorite occupation in the kindergarten, and older children are usually very fond of the work. This is noticeable when they visit the kindergarten, especially if they have passed through its course of instruction. To these children much of the kindergarten material can be given directly, for they will know how to use it, and they have at home the time and scope for invention with it which the kindergartner was perhaps unable to give.

With younger children and those who have not been in the kindergarten it will be necessary for the mother to keep the store of mats, strips and needles to herself, allowing the children to weave only on occasion or for a definite purpose. If the materials are where a child can get them at will, and if he is allowed freedom to begin several mats and finish none, the weaving will neither interest nor attract him very long, but given out as a thing to be valued and really used it may be a source of both pleasure and profit. The mothers who do not know what this weaving material is can easily learn at the kindergarten supply stores, where dealers will be glad to show them just how the work is done, and to furnish them with the catalogue containing patterns. Perhaps an easier way will be to get some kindergarten friend to outline the necessary steps, and give what other technical instruction is desired.

Most mothers of to-day, when they were children themselves, beguiled some of their leisure hours weaving small slats, which were split up from strawberry boxes, into screens, fans and the like. This should not become a lost art, and when strawberry boxes are not at hand, slats of all sizes and colors can be bought. In summer wide flags and other rushes can be braided into mats after the manner of our remoter ancestors. Educators tells us that the child develops as did the race, and, therefore, that the occupations of primitive man, the hunting, building of shelters, weaving and modeling, especially attract children.

The weaving of wide strips of colored cloth is easily accomplished with the fingers, and the result can be transformed into various useful articles, such as iron-holders and pads for handling hot stove-lifters and blowers. Several mothers have told me that the weaving of ribbon or braid in and out the holes of a cane-seated chair, by means of a tape needle, is an amusement which often lasts for long periods of time. One little girl who tried this and enjoyed it very much subsequently offered to re-seat an old chair. The bottomless chair, strong cloth strips, tacks and hammer were given her, and the result was lots of fun for the small artisan, even if the chair was not altogether safe after she had finished it.

Quite the most remarkable bit of weaving by children, which has come to my knowledge, was done by some small boys in whose play-room a painter's ladder was placed diagonally from ceiling to floor, in such a way that each end was firmly held. Through this fascinating plaything the boys were wont to weave themselves in their moments of recreation. This was only one of the many delightful things that could be done with the ladder, and it long remained a favorite among the gymnastic appliances which adorned this particular play spot.

Sand is always a favorite plaything indoors and out, but how to provide it as an indoor plaything is something of a problem. A large pan with deep sides will hold enough sand for one child to play in satisfactorily, but where there is room enough the sand table of the kindergarten may become a part of the nursery or play-room furnishing if desired. This table is variously constructed, being usually an adaptation of some table or bench already in possession. In my own case it is the plainest kind of a wash-bench, whose sides were fenced in by the janitor. Near the table hangs a dust-pan and brush, and as it is almost impossible for the children to play without spilling some sand over the edge, it has become a part of the play to sweep up. This has become such a matter of course that no one thinks anything about it, and it seems to answer the objection sure to be raised against sand in the house.

At first the child is contented to play in the sand by himself, building it into houses and fences, leveling them, patting the sand down, and doing other things of a similar nature. As long as he will so employ himself, of course no assistance in the way of suggestion is necessary, but when he reaches his limitations a very little help will often put a whole new set of operations in train. The addition of a ruler or flattened stick with which round houses can be shaped into square ones, and surfaces smoothed or trimmed down, will set the ball rolling again. Spheres, cubes, cylinders and other objects with which impressions can be made in the damp sand, should be given when the occasion calls for them. All sorts of little cups and dishes from which sand cakes can be

turned will come into play, and a sand pie
carefully made in a tin-plate or old china
saucer, is not a thing to be despised with its
ornamented crust.   When I was a child I
remember investing my pennies for a long
time in fascinating little tin-dishes shaped
like hearts, stars and other beautiful things,
and such dishes are still on sale.

When the sand is dry a set of homeo-
pathic medicine bottles will prove a treasure.
Indeed, bottles by themselves are not altogether undesirable playthings, as children
usually are fond of them and make up many
interesting plays with them.   One little
child who goes to the kindergarten was delighted to set up a kindergarten of his own
with empty bottles for pupils, in which his
children sang, marched and played as happily afternoons as he did mornings.   This
sort of representation of their own lives appeals very strongly to most little children,
and spools, clothes-pins, flowers, marbles,
pins and other objects easily serve their purpose.   They especially delight to represent
children collectively, as a school, kindergar-

ten, party or excursion. Pins and a pin-cushion will amuse a baby for a long time, where the pins are made to answer for people, animals and objects that he knows.

Returning to the sand, some of the more elaborate plays of children with this plastic material take the form of farms, gardens, parks, fairy-lands, and geographical formations. Houses, walks, fences and yards are made, trees and flowers planted, lakes and rivers excavated, and roads laid out. Representations of particular localities, the streets of a town, country roads, hills of a definite section, and the surroundings of any particular spot can be made in a sand pan. Of course the sand pile in the yard, the real lake shore, sea beach, or river bank, is preferable to a pan or table indoors, but as in our latitude we are housed more or less for eight months of the year the sand-pan has its place.

The clay sold at art stores and by kindergarten supply dealers can be used to advantage at home if the kindergarten idea of using it as a means of expression is held by the mother. The kindergartner usually has some definite object in her mind towards which the children are glad to work with her. That object is something which she knows is a part of that inner life which they are always trying to express in action. With this definite work she gives them plenty of time and opportunity to work out anything they wish—to do what they please with the clay. At home the mother knows what is most predominant in her child's thought at any particular time, and she can help him to express this very easily with clay by choosing to make with him, or have him make, some object which stands in close relation to it. One great incentive to careful work with clay is a place in which the work can be kept, comparisons made and improvement noted. So, too, is an aim in working, a gift to be made, a surprise prepared, a good-natured joke perpetrated, or a souvenir presented.

Some of the objects to which the clay most readily adapts itself are fruit, birds, nests, nuts, pods, vegetables, houses, boxes, trunks, animals, sets of dishes, kitchen and other utensils, fish, turtles, frogs, mice, etc. Whole sets of objects can be made with the ball, the half ball, the oblate spheroid, the prolate spheroid, cube, cylinder, parallelopipeds, prisms and other forms for bases.

A bird can be made with five balls, one large and four small ones. The large one becomes a body, one small one a head on which a beak is readily formed by pinching the clay into the required shape, two small balls are flattened for wings, and the last ball is similarly treated for a tail.

Another pleasant occupation is the making of a leaf plaque in repoussé work. A ball is made and flattened into a disc about a quarter of an inch thick. Upon this, rough side down, is laid a leaf. All the exposed surface is gently pricked with a wooden toothpick, after which the leaf is taken away, its clear impression remaining in the midst of the rough surface.

Impressions made in the clay with wooden blocks of various forms is commended by art teachers as suitable work for little children. These impressions can be so placed as to form borders and patterns.

At Thanksgiving time in some kindergartens cabins are built of clay logs, and often a number of children working together produce the articles which go to make up a shoe shop, bakery, blacksmith's shop, or which represent any other industry.

Try the experiment some time of letting the child tell the story of the day, his walk, a ride or any other experience, with the clay, with the direct object of making papa read the story when he comes home at night.

In the home use of all these materials each mother will use her own discretion as to whether the child is to have free access to them at all times, whether they are to be used at stated times, or whether they are to be brought out only on occasion. Each will know which way will best suit her children, their environment and her own circumstances.

A party of older children, and even grown-up people, can have a most amusing evening

with the clay.   Give to each a piece of suitable size and require some very familiar object, a head and face, a cow, a horse, a man
or anything equally well known, to be made
in a specified number of minutes and give a
prize for the one voted best.   Modeling the
human head and face, which seems the easi-
est and most familiar, generally produces
the most amusing results in a party of amateur sculptors.

Chapter VI.

WITH NEEDLE AND THREAD.

AMONG the occupations given by Froebel to his pupils for use in the kindergarten was a carefully elaborated school of pricking, beginning with straight lines and running through their various combinations, to which were added diagonals and their combinations, curves and their combinations, all of which were to lead to the invention of designs in lines and curves. This school of work has been largely discarded by the training classes on account of the straining of eyes and premature use of smaller muscles, as well as for other psychological reasons. In few, if any, of the kindergartens of to-day will one find the school of pricking in use, but the occasional pricking of simple designs and representations of objects is still used to the delight of the older children. They love to do this sort of work, and in a good light and for a short time can do it without injury.

In many homes the children at times ask for, or are given, a piece of paper or cardboard on which a picture is drawn for them to prick, and carrying out the kindergarten idea of making the work the expression of an occasion or of the child's thought, it can bring added pleasure to the satisfaction already found in the more primitive method. Any stationer will, for a small sum, cut cards of bristol board or manila paper of any desired dimension, and a store of these should be added to the nursery playthings. If economy demands it old visiting cards, advertisements and invitations may be utilized.

A pricking cushion can be easily made of two or three thicknesses of strong cloth, and a hat-pin or belt-pin will do for a needle, although the regular needle with its wooden handle, which is used in the kindergarten, is perhaps more comfortable to manipulate.

Chief among the subjects for pricking cards are the objects of interest surrounding the child at any particular time. Other simple objects especially well adapted to this particular kind of representation are fruits, vegetables, flowers, clocks, birds, animals, leaves, pods, tools, implements, utensils, fish, turtles, butterflies, stars and moon phases. Pretty borders around the edges of these pricked pictures add much to the effect as well as to the time required in producing it.

As to the difficulty in supplying the necessary designs, there are many ways of getting around one's inability to draw. Nearly everybody has at least one friend who can and will draw a picture if asked to do so; pattern objects can be cut out and used for tracing, and last, but not least, our own crude drawings do not look to the children as they do to us. Picture cards especially prepared for this occupation are sold by dealers in kindergarten supplies, and from their catalogues selections can be made in accordance with individual desires and circumstances.

These pricked cards can be made into transparencies to be hung in windows, calendars, pin-trays, letter-pockets, covers for needle-books, and many other things. They can also be pasted into a scrap-book for preservation. This scrap-book should be a part of the nursery outfit in order that work well done of many sorts may be kept. When filled, it will be a treasure always in the mother's eyes, a delight to the child himself as he grows older, perhaps a source of child-study data, and often a valued gift to some loved member of the family or distant friend.

It seems hardly necessary to add that the right side of a finished pricked picture is the rough side, and for this reason while children at home and in school often prick names, words, and sentences, such cards do not present a very satisfactory appearance when finished, as on the rough side the writing is reversed and the smooth side shows the pencil marks. Kindergartners do not recommend pricking for children under five years of age, but from that time on experience has shown them that when used wisely nature has no objections to it.

In nearly all homes little girls sew patchwork and dolls' clothes, and outline simple designs in fancy work. To this is often added the old-fashioned knitting on four pins and a spool, which delighted their elders' younger days. Instead of pins, use smooth, slender nails, and drive them in so that they are a little over half an inch high. Odds and ends of worsted please the children best, as they enjoy the frequent change of color. Shaded worsteds, I remember, we especially enjoyed, and a little shop where penny skeins could be purchased stands out clearly among my mental images.

This spool-work, when finished, can be made into reins for playing horse, as well as into mats and holders.

The "wonder ball" of modern times is one of the best gifts to a child old enough to do this knitting. A number of inexpensive trifles are rolled into the ball of worsted which is to be knit, and as the knitter works his industry is rewarded by the frequent dropping out of these concealed treasures. Sewing on real clothes for a definite object appeals more to a child than the old-fashioned "stent," given merely to teach sewing. To work on a gift for a friend, a garment for a poorer child, or something which is to be really used in the house, is not the task that sewing for its own sake is apt to become.

In the kindergarten boys as well as girls like to sew, and there is no reason why a boy should ever be deprived of this pleasure. It certainly is no disadvantage to any man to know how to sew on a button or do a bit of mending, and it certainly is a great advantage to any boy in this way to learn self-reliance, helpfulness and consideration. I know a family of four children, two boys and two girls, where each does his own mending and cares for his own room. The fact that soldiers, sailors, hunters and college men must often do their own mending appeals strongly to the average small boy, who, I have come to believe, is often really fond of this particular kind of work. I know one little lad of six who has been very anxious to learn to knit on real knitting needles ever since he learned that in Scotland many a man knows how to "click the pricks," for which bit of information we are indebted to Miss Alcott.

The kindergarten sewing is a good beginning for later and more elaborate efforts. A three-year-old can begin in this way, and it will continue to interest him until he is ten or more. There is, as in the pricking, a regular school of work, or rather, many schools more or less elaborated, consisting of lines, angles, curves and their combinations, leading to the invention of designs. Any mother can possess herself of one of these schools of work through a kindergarten friend, should she desire to do so, and for children of seven years and over she could use it to great advantage, but for home use for younger children the picture sewing will perhaps be the most desirable and available.

A store of Bristol board or stiff manila cards, about 6 × 8 inches, and a little ingenuity, will bring many a pleasant hour into the nursery. If it is practicable to paint the pictures sewed in outline, stiff water-color paper should be procured for such work. Nothing is better for the baby's first sewing lessons than the simple representations of the six kindergarten balls of red, blue, yellow, orange, green and purple. In our own kindergarten we have used in place of or sometimes after this a series consisting of a red apple, blue ball, yellow lemon, orange, green pear and purple plum. Carrying out the idea a little further, when it seems necessary, we have added a red tomato, yellow squash, green cucumber, orange pumpkin and purple egg plant. In this work the objects should be as large as life size when practicable; the needle, coarse, and the stitches, long.

The list of objects given for the pricked pictures is equally good for sewing, and to these should be added, as in other cases, the objects occupying the child's thought at the time, as, for instance, an outlined mitten just before it is time to put on winter clothing; for it is then, as I well remember, that a child's mind is full of anticipatory visions of sleds, skates, snow-storms and winter sports generally, all of which ideas he should be helped to express in various ways, of which sewing is one. As further instances, a stocking at Christmas time, a big fire-cracker before the Fourth of July, a trunk when a journey is contemplated, are suggested.

In any kindergarten supply catalogue a large number of illustrations of picture-sewing cards will be found. These may be bought, copied, or used suggestively when new material is needed.

This work must be used in some way if the children are to retain their interest in it and to have a continued incentive to further effort. It is well early in the year to set up a "Christmas box," to which all good work may be consigned to await the time when, with a very little additional labor, each piece may be transformed into a gift. The suggestions for the disposition of pricking-cards are equally applicable to the sewing-cards. All through the year birthday and other gifts for friends and relatives will furnish an output for these home industries, and the scrap-book is always at hand. There should never, from the child's point of view, be any work done just for the sake of doing it, and in a wisely administered nursery government there will be no odds and ends of work lying about as disregarded rubbish, neither will there be any careless or unfinished work.

Chapter VII.

WITH PASTE AND SCISSORS.

FOR years we have been in the habit of saying to the children in our homes, "Now run away and play!" taking it for granted that their resources and inventive powers are inexhaustible. We have often left out of account the lively little mind which demanded scope for activity as well as the body, thinking it all sufficient if the children were physically active. We have forgotten, or we never knew, that real play must have thought for its vitalizing force. By helping the children so to vitalize their play we give them additional power as well as additional pleasure. For instance, children like to cut out pictures—let us give them a reason for cutting them out! They like to cut objects out of paper free-hand—let us help them to select and classify these objects, and to do

something with them, something which
shall stimulate to further effort! They like
to paste—but "what shall I paste?" they
say. Sometimes, as has been said, we must
join in this play-work ourselves; at other
times a suggestion, a starting point, a
thought will be sufficient to keep the children busy for a long time.

For the work to be discussed in this chapter blunt pointed scissors, not too small, paper and paste, are the essentials. The paper
is of various kinds—newspaper, wrapping
paper, colored paper, paper saved from pack-
ages, kindergarten folding paper, and for
great occasions, sheets of gold and silver
paper.

The best and the cheapest paste for family
use is made of gum tragacanth and water.
Its advantages over other pastes are many.
Flour and water paste is hard on carpets,
mucilage is too sticky and the various
library pastes, snow flake pastes and the like,
while excellent for special purposes, are expensive, apt to dry up, and usually leave a
flake or crust wherever a particle is dropped.

The gum tragacanth can be bought in bulk at drug stores and twenty-five cents' worth will last for months. Half a dozen pieces dropped into a cup or bottle of water over night will make a paste which is not sticky on the fingers, which leaves no spots on clothes or carpets, and which can be kept so thick that it will not run when its receptacle is overturned. It is best to make a small quantity every two weeks or so, as it spoils if kept too long. The thinnest of the kindergarten slats make good paste brushes, as they are so inexpensive that the losing of one is a small matter, and, as we all know, brushes will get themselves lost frequently.

From the advertising leaves of our numberless magazines, illustrated papers, circulars, advertisements and old magazines the children can cut out pictures by the bushel, but they must have an object for cutting, which shall stimulate them not only to cut neatly, but to keep on cutting. Try providing a large and attractive looking box with a picture and the inscription "*For cutout pictures,*" on its cover. Explain to your small folks that all neatly cut-out pictures are to go into it, and that when you have time and there are enough pictures you and they will make a good use of the contents. Say that you need a great many pictures, and make your purpose a mystery, or tell the whole story as you see fit. When a sufficent quantity of pictures has accumulated take time to look them over with the children, if they cannot do it alone, and sort them into all kinds of groups—little boy pictures, little girl pictures, work pictures, play pictures, cat pictures, dog pictures, any one kind of animal pictures, indoor pictures, outdoor pictures, summer pictures, winter pictures, farm pictures, city pictures, country pictures, baby pictures, water pictures, and any others you may need or want. From these make up classified scrap-books, animal books, children books, outdoor books, indoor books, and so on. Make the scrap-books of cambric or strong wrapping paper, label them conspicuously on the outside, and then let them be presented to baby relations and neighbors, poor children who have few or no picture books, free kindergartens and hospital wards. Do not make these presentations yourself, but let the children do it, that they may have the pleasure of seeing the outcome of their labors.

Cut out the tops and bottoms of large pasteboard boxes, hang them up by a cord or ribbon, let the children invent some kind of a pretty border to go around the edges, and on them mount groups of classified pictures. These charts make good gifts for sick-rooms, where they can be hung in sight of the bed or couch. They should be filled on both sides. In cutting out some pictures it is better to cut out the object or objects instead of preserving the whole picture. Animals cut out in this way can be made to prowl over a chart in a most interesting fashion.

Large pictures can be pasted on the tops or bottoms of boxes of suitable size and then cut up into puzzles for little invalids. The colored art supplements which our newspapers lavish upon us are good for this purpose.

Among the kindergarten supplies are envelopes filled with paper circles, squares and triangles which may become home treasures if rightly used. A pasting-book can be improvised or bought for five cents. In this the child can make a red page, a blue page, and yellow, orange, green and purple pages, by neatly pasting one square or circle in each alternate squared space, or by arranging a number of them in any other desired and orderly fashion. On subsequent pages he can invent borders and designs, keeping always in mind that symmetry, proportion and regularity are necessary to good results. Let him lay his border or design before beginning to paste it, and let all suggestions and corrections be made then.

By cutting colored paper into short strips, material for kindergarten chains can be made at home. These the children will of their own accord paste by the yard, but they yield much more profit and pleasure if pasted with some regard to color and number, two red and two blue, three yellow and three orange, and so on. Chains of six colors put together in the order of the colors of the spectrum are very pleasing, and the variety of big chains, little chains, middle-sized chains, and chains whose links are of different sizes will afford scope and variety to the work. These chains have the best excuse for being made when the decoration of nursery, sitting room or piazza for some great occasion is in order. They also make fine military trappings for small soldiers.

If children can be led up to any degree of skill in free-hand cutting an endless vista will open before them. We are all familiar with those prodigies whose work is exhibited at fairs and expositions, but between this and the baby's first crude cutting of scraps there is every degree of proficiency. I call to mind one little boy of five or six whose scissors produced most remarkable bugs and insects, and whose sister at about the same age cut very good heads of animals. Another child in the same family invented sets of dishes, while another ran entirely to dolls. A family of boys cut out on one occasion an entire circus procession, which was the admiration of several generations. The possibilities of free-hand cutting are great, but it must be borne in mind that crude beginnings lead up to excellent results, and that the day of small things must not be despised. It is something to know how to handle scissors at all; it is an advance to slit up any oblong piece of paper and call it a "pair of pants," as one three-year-old used to do. To lead children to take pleasure in this occupation if they do not, as we say, "take to it naturally;" that is, indulge in it freely of their own accord, it is necessary to appreciate their efforts, to show them how they can improve, and to give them an object for cutting. They will very often cut contentedly for long periods of time just for the sake of cutting, but there are also times when with an object in view their scissors will furnish pleasure and occupation, when without it they would not.

A blank book, however cheap, or one simply home-made, labeled "*Cuttings,*" in which all worthy of preservation, either because of the earnest effort which went into its making or because of a remote resemblance to the thing copied, can be kept and will furnish this object. It may for a time be necessary to write the name of the cutting underneath it for the enlightenment of interested beholders, but this to the child is an addition to rather than a detraction from his handiwork.

Charts can also be made of these cuttings, and the grouping of them into classes or sets gives a definiteness to the thought behind the results which will lead to still better performances. I have seen such charts filled with cut-out fruits, leaves and flowers, sets of dishes, tools, implements, and objects illustrating stories told or read. Houses for humans, birds, pigeons and dogs; barns, corn-cribs, fences, ladders, flags, moons, stars, boats, animals and people are some of the things which cut out well.

A clothes-line of string can be filled with the family garments hung out to dry, for which interesting industry it will be necessary to invent a clothes-pin of some sort. An oblong bit of cardboard with a slit in it is the simplest yet on record.

One group of children played shoe-store for days, first making purses of folded paper, and then cutting out money. They cut out shoes of every imaginable shape and size and arranged them for the retail trade, which flourished apace, for when their money was spent these fortunate purchasers had only to make more.

Any kind of a shop could be stocked in this way, and there never yet was a child who did not like to play store. The common pin-wheel is familiar to every one. I have a recollection, somewhat hazy, of what seemed to me a most impressive and beautiful sight known as a "pin-wheel store." There were in it pin-wheels of every size and color, and crossed sticks on which two or more pin-wheels were fastened. These were sold for pins by some older children to us younger ones.

The making of large paper flags, shields, pennons, knightly banners and signals has kept many a small boy happy indoors when he could not go out. Webster's unabridged dictionary contains numbers of flags and signals which may be learned and copied to good advantage. One little lad in whose kindergarten the knights were known and loved, beguiled the tedious hours of a week's illness by making banners. He not only cut out and mounted the banners on sticks, but invented endless objects and devices which he pasted upon them. He branched out from these to a George Washington banner, which he made of a large piece of brown paper and covered with pictures and cuttings appropriate to the subject. He was at the time just five years old. Two years later he put in his time on Washington's Birthday, when he had of course no school, in making the United States shield out of pasteboard, paper, and gold stars, purchased from choice with his own money.

The old-fashioned paper dolls which gave us grown-ups so much pleasure in our youthful days have been largely superseded by those ready made for sale, but the pleasure I myself took and the occupation I found in making my own ought to be experienced by other children. To cut out your own family of dolls, regulating number, size and sex to suit yourself, painting their faces, heads and feet, and then clothing them in garments fashioned after the prevailing modes, by means of a brush and colors, is a most absorbingly interesting occupation. In this connection I recall making my own paint-brushes at times out of quill tooth-picks and fur from the cat. Peach-box houses, with additions made of other boxes as the family increases, furnished with paper furniture of your own making, water colors and etchings by yourself, carpets and curtains from your mother's piece-bag are all joy-producing instruments.

Few children who come to the kindergarten know how to cut out paper dolls at all, and none have any idea of dressing them, but I have never yet tried to teach a child to do this who was not delighted with the work.

In the scrapbook to which the free-hand cuttings are consigned, any pretty bits of folding can also be preserved. If the children go to the kindergarten they will, after they have had enough experience in folding, be delighted to fold at home with the regularly prepared papers or those which they form into squares themselves. If this latter course is pursued they must be able to make their squares exact by means of a ruler. If they do not go to a kindergarten it will be an immense help to the mother to get one of her kindergarten friends to give her the "school of folding" for use with her children. These friends often feel a little delicate about proffering services which may not be welcome, but they will gladly give any assistance in their power, which is really *wanted*. Written directions for this work are not very satisfactory and would of necessity be tediously long. The work needs to be done to be really learned. Folding-papers 4x4, 5x5 and 6x6 are used in the kindergartens. At home the children will take pleasure in reproducing their kindergarten folding in papers of a larger size as 8x8, 10x10 or 12x12. Large boats, chickens and ducks of different sizes, families of pigs, sleds and furniture are a few of the things which can be charmingly made with folding paper.

In one of our kindergartens the children use a news paper for several kinds of cutting. They like to have it when they want to do a particularly large piece of work; they use it for experimenting before cutting into the finer papers, for patterns, and for games like the shoe-store when nothing else could be had in sufficient quantity.

On one occasion each child made a baker's cup, apron and cuffs for himself. All the small workmen then joined in the baker's parade through the primary schoolrooms, throwing oyster-crackers, to an appreciative populace, with a lavish hand, as they marched.

Before leaving the subject let me call to mind a little soldier who paraded up and down our street one afternoon having a beautiful time with himself. He wore a paper-cap of his own making which was gay with tassels and fringe. Paper-chains were festooned over his martial breast and fell in streamers from his shoulders and at his side. He carried a paper-flag which he had made, presenting altogether a very striking appearance, and he was evidently very happy.

Chapter VIII.

WITH PAINTS AND PENCILS.

NOTHING brings such peace and harmony into a family as the lead pencil, and any help given to a child which will enable him to engage in artistic pursuits is a boon to him and all his relatives. It is astonishing in view of this fact how few mothers think it worth while to keep in the house good paper and decently sharpened pencils. We have but to go back into our own childhood to realize how much greater is the pleasure of writing or drawing with a good pen or pencil than with a poor one, and on good paper instead of poor paper. We grown-ups have access at all times to good materials and have perhaps forgotten how it feels to write with a blunt pencil on a piece of crumpled wrapping paper, hence the necessity of backward chronological excursions occasionally.

Two little girls who were fond of drawing were furnished by their father with large, good blank books and sharp pencils. The hours of quiet enjoyment which they passed were only a part of the good results which followed. There was the increased skill which practice gave, the growth of the imaginative faculties, and the pleasure which grown-up friends and relatives took in looking over the books, as they often did evenings after the children were in bed. The mother of course saw the pictures as they were drawn, and commended effort whenever it seemed wise to do so, but most of the pictures were so irresistibly funny that she only allowed friends to see them when the children were not present.

Another mother started a similar book for her four-year-old son, labeling the objects drawn according to his direction, and it is needless to say that that finished volume will be a treasured one.

The artistic mother of a lively little lad fell into the habit of drawing a picture for him every evening, he furnishing all ideas and suggestions as to what should be drawn. Two blank books full of these sketches were treasures in that family for years, and may be yet for aught I know. A large family of brothers and sisters in one of our public schools showed such remarkable proficiency in drawing that one of the teachers asked the mother how it happened that they were all talented instead of one or two, as is usual in families where there is any talent at all. She replied that drawing was one of their favorite occupations at home, and that in the evening a common amusement for the whole family was to set some object in the middle of the dining-room table, which each drew to the best of his ability.

Many of our public schools do such good work in drawing that the children are full of school ideas which they would be glad to work out at home had they the materials. The younger children need these materials as well as the older ones, to prepare them for the public school work which is ahead of them, as well as for other and obvious reasons.

The reproduction of stories told and read with the pencil is an unfailing resource in school, and could be at home. The illustration of home happenings of interest, of anticipated pleasures, and of past enjoyments should be added to the list of subjects for and incentives to pencil work. An additional picture drawn in an appreciated drawing book with a good pencil is a very different thing to the child from an illustration on the back of an old envelope, drawn with the stub of a pencil, and destined within twenty-four hours to be thrown into the waste basket.

The home blackboard has come to be an institution. Colored crayons added to the store of white chalk will bring a new interest into this particular play, but children, if left entirely to themselves, soon reach their limitations even with a possession so enjoyed as colored chalk. One mother has tried with success the experiment of keeping this artistic weapon in her own possession and giving it out as a reward of merit for any particularly good white drawing, which of course speedily becomes a colored one. Fruits, vegetables and leaves lend themselves readily to representation with chalk, as does any other object of simple outline. Illustrations of stories, and copies of the objects laid with sticks, seeds or tablets are suggestive for home blackboard work, as well as pictures designed to represent specific objects.

In answer to the question, " What shall I draw ? " one may suggest among other things an apple-tree, the clock, a bird-house, a tree whose leaves are falling, cats, dogs, barns, fences, ladders, houses, farm implements, a kitchen, parlor, dining-room, bedroom, Thanksgiving picture, winter picture with lots of snow coming down, Eskimo scene, day picture, night picture, Christmastree stockings, chimney, fire-place, carpenter work, blacksmith work, logging camp, bakery, mills, sheep, windy day, rainy day, the ocean full of fishes, boats, and so on. For colored chalk besides the fruits, vegetables, leaves and flowers there are the colored balls, the spectrum, flags of all nations, signal and yachting flags, college banners, and baseball caps.

Draw the things in season, as sleds in November, " what you want " before Christmas, parasols in May and a cannon for Fourth-of-July. The same general rule for working out the child's thought and inner life applies here as elsewhere.

Water colors may be used for the same work on a smaller scale as the colored chalk, and to it may be added the coloring of sewing cards, good pencil drawings, the woodcuts in the hospital and other scrap books, and the paper dolls previously mentioned.

Teach the children, if they do not find out for themselves, which would be better, that red and yellow mixed will make orange color; blue and yellow, green; crimson-lake and Prussian blue, purple; that white mixed with crimson-lake will make pink, with Prussian blue, light blue; with black, gray; that black added to any color will make it darker, and white lighter. The ignorance of these simple facts shown by grown up assistants in the kindergarten shows plainly how many children pass through childhood without finding out what they can do with paints and brushes.

The stencil cards sold by dealers in school supplies are good materials for home use. These pictures can be painted when finished. The cards are also to be found in sizes large enough for blackboard use.

Painting or drawing the leaves, grasses, flowers, weeds and seed-pods, when once taught a child, gives him an inexhaustible resource and is not so difficult of acquirement as one would think. The best drawing teachers have even the youngest school children draw and paint directly from the object, and prefer for them the natural objects of simple outlines and vivid colorings, as for instance, the Hubbard and crookneck squashes, gourds, yellow and green cucumbers, sprays of pine, radishes, cherries, parrots' feathers, and so forth. There is of course no end of such objects and they are to be found everwhere. Little children like to trace around an object and over a picture on tissue paper, and while all such outlining and tracing is discouraged by art teachers for older children, the little ones, who are learning to use their own hands as well as pencils and brushes, may safely indulge in it.

Cut out circles, squares, oblongs and triangles from stiff paper and the younger children will trace pages of them. They will welcome the suggestion of a definite something to draw inside of these figures, they will also enjoy making borders in this way and coloring them.

The traced outline of the child's own little hand makes a good Christmas card or design for a scrap-book cover. Leaves can be traced, colored, cut out and borders made of them. Pattern objects cut out of cards, papers, or books can be used in this way. A paper picture selected as suitable for tracing should be pasted on a card before being cut out. A child can trace pictures of wild geese and flying birds which will make pretty wall decorations for his own room. Bronze or maroon paper is best for this.

Chapter IX.

CHRISTMAS AND HOLIDAY WORK.

THE Christmas box mentioned in the preceding pages should be an institution all the year round. Every good bit of work which has no other purpose to serve can be laid away in it and a certain day appointed for its opening, which ought to be a ceremony and an occasion. When its contents are spread out there will be displayed many articles which can easily be transformed into iron and blower holders, covers for needle books, penwipers, blotters, memorandum books, backgrounds for calendars, book-marks, satchet packets, hair receivers, mats, pin-trays, Christmas cards, match scratchers and the many other articles which individual ingenuity will invent. A long list of friends and relatives can be remembered in this way, and the Christmas money so economized can be spent for Christmas greens, fascinating tree decorations, and unexpected temptations to festivity. A little paste, paper, paint, sachet powder, worsted and ribbon will do wonders, and the odds and ends of baby ribbon, and other kinds as well, which accumulate in a year's time, will answer all purposes so well that the expense of twenty Christmas presents will be almost nothing, and the child's own handiwork the chief part of the gift.

The joy of the Christmas season lies as largely in the preceeding weeks of preparation and anticipation as in the day of giving and receiving. I well remember how as soon as Thanksgiving had passed we children began to draw Christmas pictures and to repeat to ourselves and each other the ever-thrilling "'T was the night before Christmas!" Do not be afraid of letting the little folks begin too soon on their Christmas work, for there will be much to do. They can work for many afternoons and evenings on tree trimmings alone. Experience has taught many of us that children of six and over enjoy trimming a tree for others much more than being surprised on Christmas morning by one carefully prepared for them by some one else. It will be easy to find people for whom a tree can be decorated. The many poorer and less fortunate children in any public school, kindergarten or neighborhood, can be had for the asking. Even grown-up folks like to be invited to a Christmas tree; and I remember four small people who secretly bought and dressed a tree with which they completely surprised their father and mother when they entered the dining room on Christmas morning.

For tree trimmings nothing is more satisfactory to the children who are fortunate enough to be allowed to do their own work than the paper chains of the kindergarten. For this occasion these should be of gold and silver as well as colored paper. They can be made coarse or fine, according to the age of the children, and superfluous quantities may be utilized as decorations for the room in which the tree is to be placed. The chains made of small circles, squares and triangles in conjunction with one-inch straws are very effective.   These should be hung upside down, so that the colored side of the paper will show, and here, too, gold and silver paper can be used to advantage.

Pretty gold, silver and colored hollow cubes, to be filled with popcorn or candy, can be made by pasting six, five or six-inch papers together, each of which is folded thus:

Fold the front edge to the back. Open.

Fold the right edge to the left. Open.

Fold each corner to the middle. Turn over.

Fold each corner to the middle again.

Cornucopias can be made of folding paper thus:

Fold the front corner to the back.   Open.

Fold one edge to the middle line.

Fold the adjacent long edge to the middle line.

The result is a trapezium. Fold the right isosceles triangle at the top, over the two right scalene triangles, and you will have an acute isosceles triangle. Three of these pasted together make a good receptacle for candy or popcorn. The outside can be decorated with paint, strips of paper or scrap pictures. Worsted or ribbon is needed to make loops for hanging the cornucopias on the tree and for the lower end.

For two weeks before the twenty-fifth have the eggs used in the house, whenever it is possible, broken open at one end and the shells carefully saved. When these shells are painted with luster-paint, filled with popcorn, and hung up by loops of worsted passed through two inch paper tops, which are cut into fanciful shapes, they rival the glass balls sold in the stores.

When we were children we covered egg shells with strips of colored paper, but the luster-paint is an improvement on that more primitive method. The gold stars and other tiny objects sold for progressive euchre purposes decorate the shells beautifully.

Nuts, cones and other trifles can also be painted with this luster-paint as well as the apples often necessary to weigh down the lower and heavier branches of the tree. Strings of popcorn and cranberries will always hold their own places, as will tiny flags, sachet bags and Japanese trifles. A paper lantern, which makes a pretty decoration, is easily constructed if one folds the two long edges of an oblong piece of paper together. Holding the closed edge down, slit up the entire piece to within quarter of an inch of the top edge. Open and paste the two short edges together. Let the slit pieces be as fine as possible and the paper about 4x5 or 5x6. A handle is pasted on, by means of which the little lantern is hung upon the tree.

A Christmas number of one of our educational journals gave the following directions for making Christmas snow balls:

Make a small paper cube and fill it with popcorn.

Fold a piece of soft white cotton around it. Wind this on with white yarn, using only enough to hold the cotton in place. With a crochet needle gently pull out the cotton between the layers of yarn until the ball is round, white and fluffy, then powder the ball with diamond dust.

Sprays of pine and spruce dipped into a solution of alum, which is allowed to crystallize on the needles, is another Christmas suggestion.

The uses of this child-decorated tree are many. It is a fitting spot for Santa Claus' operations, a place prepared for him. It is a celebration of the day in itself. It can be a joy to the eye for a week, and, best of all, as has been hinted, it can be shared with friends and neighbors, every family answering for itself the question, "And who is my neighbor?"

Christmas cards decorated with the child's own sewing, pricking, printing or other handiwork, which is arranged as seems best around one of the many reproductions of famous Nativity pictures, which can be cut out of old December magazines, are worth having and keeping. A gilded star in an upper corner adds to its suggestiveness.

A Christmas tree for the cat is great fun on the day before Christmas. Bits of raw meat and bunches of catnip are the most acceptable gifts, but tiny balls on the ends of the branches make good cat playthings

A sparrow's Christmas tree is best made of a sheaf of oats garnered for the purpose in the Fall, but in default of this a sympathetic mother and imaginative children can easily devise a substitute, as sparrows are not at all exclusive in their tastes.

The reading of Christmas tales during the preceding days and week, the learning of Christmas verses and the singing of Christmas songs add both to the joy of the occasion and the real Christmas spirit which every mother desires to foster in her child.

"The Birds' Christmas Carol," by Kate Douglas Wiggin, is full of Christmas suggestions which children delight to carry out, if encouraged to do so.

HALLOWE'EN.

To this old-time festival the children fondly cling, as it appeals strongly to their imaginations. The real origin of the e'en is not very clear even in grown-up minds, and little children can be made best to understand it through the medium of the Brownies. Thanks to Palmer Cox, the Brownies are known and loved by all the children in the land, and when they are told that long ago the people believed that on Hallowe'en these little creatures came out and played pranks, they have no difficulty in taking in the situation. They can also be told of the helpful Brownies made known to us by George Macdonald and Miss Mulock, and they will readily welcome the idea of secretly doing some kind or helpful thing to some one in the hope that he will think the Brownies have been at work. Two little boys of my acquaintance invented a Brownie game which is a boon to their respective families. They put on their felt slippers and amuse themselves trying to see how close they can come to different members of the family without being seen. If discovered they run like lightning back to their hole which is in some mysteriously hidden spot.

Weird little Brownies can be made with pins, peanuts and a little black paint. Real jack o' lanterns made of pumpkins and rep-resentations of them with paint, paper or worsted are in order on the last day of October, and these efforts can be sent in all sorts of mysterious fashions to friends and neighbors. Good-natured pranks and jokes ought to be met with sympathy, and it does me good to remember that on last Hallowe'en a father, mother, sister and brother all helped the five-year-old of the family to get their Jersey calf up on a neighbor's porch by way of a surprise.

Older children love to frolic in sheets and pillow-cases, pull candy, duck for apples, sail nutshell boats with fortune-telling candles aboard, and go through the list of all the tricks they know. Perhaps a variety would be a real Brownie party, if any one cared to take the trouble, where each child was dressed like one of the Brownies in the picture-books.

WASHINGTON'S BIRTHDAY.

A programme carried out at a recent Washington party given for boys and girls may be of interest in this connection.

The house was decorated with flags, and tiny flag souvenirs bearing the name and the date were made ready to pin upon each guest as he arrived. The first game was "Mixed Quotations." A number of patriotic sentiments were written on slips of cardboard and these, cut into two or more pieces, were thrown in a heap upon a table about which all could gather. Flag prizes were given to those putting rightly together the greatest number.

"Twisted Words" followed. Each child received a card on which was written:

1. Reorgge Nostginhaw.
2. Hetryecrer.
3. Lidores.
4. Areglen.
5. Diprentes.
6. Clawsilnor.
7. Hibstir.
8. Iranamec.
9. Studesatiten.
10. Kumest.
11. Dowrs.
12. Vononmentur.

These letters when placed in their proper position spell:

1. George Washington.
2. Cherry Tree.
3. Soldiers.
4. General.
5. President.
6. Cornwallis.
7. British.
8. American.
9. United States.
10. Musket.
11. Sword.
12. Mount Vernon.

A certain time was allowed for twisting the words into their own shapes and flag prizes again awarded.

After this a patriotic story was read to the children by a grown-up friend, and then all the songs of home and country known by the children were sung. Preserved cherries and Washington cake were served, and the party was over by nine o'clock.

Another set of boys and girls who had learned many of our best national songs at school, with a sympathetic friend of the educational pursuasion, took advantage of the good sleighing to go serenading on the twenty-second. The warm welcomes which they received and the various adventures they had would take up in recital more space than these pages can afford. As many of our schools are now conducted a patriotic concert given to mothers, fathers and friends is easily carried through, as a very little rehearsing of school songs is the only requisite for a musical entertainment well worth listening to in any ordinary neighborhood.

OTHER HOLIDAYS.

For Thanksgiving Day, New Year's Day and Memorial Day, pretty souvenirs can be made of the pricking and sewing cards. Pumpkins, turkeys, log cabins and Mayflowers can be easily drawn for the children, as well as mottoes, New Year bells, flags, cannon and monuments.

A turn can be given April fool jokes which will bring pleasure to the giver and receiver; for a joke in its true inwardness is a surprise, and surprises can be made kindly as well as disagreeable.

Material for birthday presents may be always at hand in an industrious household, with much love and good will worked into them by the little fingers.

Easter eggs can be fashioned after the manner of the Christmas egg-shell as well as the old-fashioned dyeing processes. Numbers of all kinds of eggs hidden about house or grounds on Easter morning will be a delight to small hunters. Encourage them to prepare and give away Easter eggs and Easter cards.

Chapter X.

GAMES AND PLAYS.

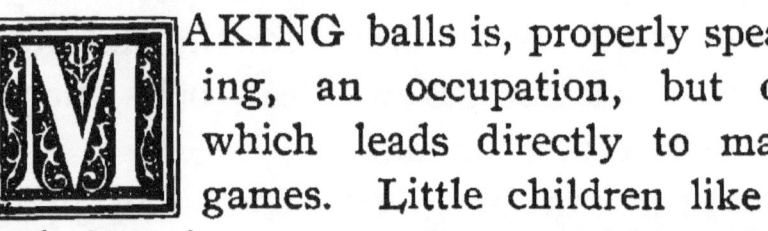MAKING balls is, properly speaking, an occupation, but one which leads directly to many games. Little children like to feel that they can make something which may really be used and for this reason enjoy making balls in the primitive fashion here suggested. A piece of old cloth of any or a desired color is snipped with the scissors along one edge, ready for tearing, the cuts being about half an inch apart. The child tears the cloth into narrow strips, seeming greatly to enjoy the sound and the process generally. These strips he ties together and winds into a ball. If over this he can wind some coarse yarn and if his mother will fasten the end for him, he will have made a very good plaything.

Six of these in the six standard colors will, in connection with a good kindergarten music book, furnish material for many happy plays for the little child whose mother will take the trouble to learn the ball games and songs.

The cloth ball can even be made large enough for an amateur football if one is desired, and soft balls uncovered by yarn will make good missiles for throwing at a home-made target. Crumpled newspaper balls also make good material for projectile purposes.

The simple game of catching the ball would not be so overlooked in the nursery if mothers could see the differences which exist in trained and untrained hands where many children are compared as they can be in the kindergarten. Everything which adds to a child's skill and dexterity is of help to him physically and mentally, and the little hands which can toss up a ball and catch it usually belong to the possessors of wide-awake minds.

Teach the children to catch balls, by playing with them yourself, and by encouraging them to play with each other or alone. Invent some simple system of scoring the catches and let the children display their skill to appreciative fathers and uncles. Bounding the ball is a game which calls for a rubber or a tennis ball. There are in this play two modes of procedure, bounding from the floor up and from the walls down to the hands. For the youngest children an improvised incline upon which the ball can be thrown that it may roll down into the waiting hands is suggested by Froebel.

In the kindergarten when the children are allowed to play freely with balls it is interesting to note the delight they take in simply rolling a ball over the floor and chasing it, in throwing it up without any idea of catching it, and in rolling it back and forth from one child to another. The inspiration of numbers evidently has something to do with this, for at home such amusements would not last very long, hence directed ball-play becomes necessary.

A barn built of blocks into which balls can be rolled makes a good nursery game, as does a tunnel through which, or a bridge over which cows, horses, pigs, elephants or any other creatures may pass, these of course being represented by balls.

Hiding games, where a hidden ball becomes a lost cow or sheep which must be found, is a favorite, and rolling one ball at others placed in a row, is another. When blue, for instance, is knocked out by red, blue becomes the roller and red goes into the row. Froebel taught his kindergartners to substitute the children themselves for the balls in games where such substitution is possible. The hiding game is easily transferred from the balls to the children, and the addition of a tiny bell tinkled by the lost one for guidance of the seekers is much appreciated.

The bird games so much in favor in the kindergarten can be played at home by simply imitating the observed life of the real birds, the canary, the pigeon and the sparrow. Let the small human canaries build a cage out of chairs, sticks and shawls and live a canary life inside, with crackers, water and some substitute for seed. Let the pigeons fly in and out of an improvised pigeon house, and the sparrows build their nests in a sheltered spot. With a normal, rightly developed imagination a child ought to be able to imitate the animal life which he sees about him in a way to furnish any amount of play material. In the development of this imagination a little help from the adult goes a long way, and to meet the child on his own chosen ground and act as if he really was a sparrow or a pigeon is to add to his power as well as to his pleasure.

Horse games will always be played spontaneously, but in addition to trotting in harness and drawing small vehicles there are games of galloping horses, wild horses, and hurdle-jumping horses, which are the best of fun and exercise.

At Christmas time eight children or eight chairs harnessed up for Santa Claus' reindeer, especially with a sleigh-bell accompaniment in a darkened room, is dramatic to a degree. One young Santa Claus improvised a chimney of tables and chairs down and up which he scrambled to the intense delight of his playfellows supposedly asleep on an old quilt in a corner.

One mother told me of a coalman play which delighted each of her four children in turn. A tiny iron shovel, the button-bag and a coal chute made of a long pasteboard box, were the simple materials which made a most attractive play. She also allowed her children to spread papers on the floor and play with real coal, picking out the tiny pieces of the right size for filling a little coal bucket, and chopping up the larger pieces with a small iron hatchet. The result of course was very black hands and faces, but beaming smiles and often a joyous, "See, mamma, I'm just like a real coalman!"

For groups of children gathered together at parties, picnics, on summer evenings and rainy afternoons there are many plays suggested by the kindergarten for home use.

One of the games chosen over and over again is:

"Roll over, come back!
So merry and free,
My playfellow dear,
Who shares in my glee!"

The children sit in a circle and one child from the center rolls the ball, usually a wooden one, to each of the children in turn, all singing the song. Later two children roll from the center, then three and finally four. This requires quick wits and close attention and never seems to pall. The words can be easily set to home music, but Eleanor Smith's song book No. 2 contains the most satisfactory tune we have yet had. Bean bags, with the accompanying board with a hole in it, or used simply for tossing in the old-fashioned game of "Teacher," should be revived once every so often. To play "Teacher," all stand in a row or class, the teacher and the one at the head being chosen by counting out, and the others ranked in the same way. The teacher tosses the bag to each in turn and whoever misses goes to the foot, which of course causes those below to move up one. If the teacher misses he goes to the foot and the head one becomes teacher.

Marching with bean bags on the head and ruling out each one who allows his bag to fall off makes a good game, the strife being to see who can keep marching longest. If music can be added to this game it is of course improved.

A ring or figure on the carpet into which balls or marbles must be rolled can be the basis of a game if some sort of scoring is added. The system of counting on an archery target is a suggestion for this.

The guessing games of the kindergarten deserve a place in the home as the children never seem to get enough of them. Objects for guessing may be chosen at haphazard or carefully selected. They may be guessed by feeling, by tasting, by smelling. The sense game of hearing has many forms, but its pussy-cat interpretation is perhaps the favorite. A blindfolded child stands in the middle of a ring, while the others circle around with or without music. When he raps on the floor with his cane or stick all are motionless and silent until the cane points at somebody who must take it and meow three times. We have in this way played dogs, horses, cows and other animals, as well as simply guessing a voice as it said "good morning." Sometimes a blinded child waits until another leaves the circle. Opening his eyes he guesses who is gone. This game is played with balls, fruits, nuts or any set of objects. One can easily imagine how interesting sense games of taste and smell may become without any further amplification of the subject.

Another favorite in Eleanor Smith's song book No. 2 reads:

> "Did you ever see a lassie
> Do this way and that?"

This is a very old friend in a new dress, and it is deservedly a friend, for it gives scope for any amount of ingenuity and originality. I remember seeing it played in a kindergarten, which happily was carpeted, where to the amazement of the director the little leader lay down on the floor, wrapped her skirts about her, and rolled over and over till she reached the side of the room. It is worthy of note that the teacher rolled, too.

The old hide-the-thimble game may become hide the child, the ball, the nut or anything else, but it is best with music played loudly or softly as the occasion demands. A small object may be hidden in the hands of children, seated in a row or in a circle, which is to be found with only the help of the music.

For the squirrel game all stand in a circle but two little squirrels, who have a hole away off by themselves somewhere. As the words are sung, or without them, one squirrel runs out and touching somebody's clasped hands leads him a lively chase before running back to the hole. If he is caught he is put inside the ring which is supposedly a cage, and the one who caught him becomes a squirrel. When two or more are caught they are fed nuts and then set free.

A weaving play in use in the kindergarten makes a pretty party game. The children march single file in a circle. Then falling into pairs they march for a moment two by two, they halt and form two rings, an inside and outside ring. Those outside join hands

but do not make a ring, as the leader in-
tends to weave this living strip in and out of
the inside ring, where hands are not joined.
As she weaves all sing to the old tune of
"Nellie Bly,"

> "Over one, under one,
>   Over one again.
> Under one, over one,
>   Then we do the same.
> Hi, weavers, Ho, weavers,
>   Come and weave with me!
> You'll scarcely find a happier band,
>   In all the land than we!"

The weaving may become more and more
complicated as different leaders are chosen,
as:

> Over one, under two, etc.,
> Over three, under three, etc.,
> Over one, under two, etc.,
> Over three, under one, etc.

There is an old fishing game which has
been successfully played where there are not
too many children. The fisherman sits
blindfolded in a high chair with his rod and
line in hand. Each child takes the name
of a fish, and, as they all swim about, one

at a time takes hold of the line and gently pulls it. If the fisherman can rightly guess what kind of a fish is nibbling at his bait he may become a fish while the one caught takes his place. This is not a kindergarten game but one which we used to play with Blindman's Buff, puss in the corner, still pond and hop-scotch, good games all of them. A pretty kindergarten march which might be used at parties is as follows: All march around one by one, divide at a given point and come up two by two. Divide again and come up four by four. March in a circle four by four. Fours change into tiny circles and all dance round and round. March by fours again. Inside children take hold of the dress of the leader, who stands in the middle, and run around like the spokes of a wheel. March by fours again, divide into twos, into ones, and all dance away to seats.

Trade marches, where one trade after another is represented by gestures, marching with the hands in different and changing positions, flying, skipping, galloping, trotting or wading are all suggestive for home purposes. The simple dancing games of the kindergarten can often be managed when anything more difficult or elaborate is out of the question.

To gallop-music let one child choose a partner and dance around the room, first one way and then the other; both choose partners and the four dance in the same way; four becomes eight and eight sixteen, and so on until all are dancing.

The old shaker-dance beginning, "I put my right hand in !" is easy to learn, and a skipping dance where the hippitty-hop step is used instead of the gallop, and where the children hold their partners by one hand instead of two, can be danced like the gallop dance.

To the tune of "Pop goes the weasel," or any other equally lively tune, joining hands in a ring, go to the center and back once; to the center and back twice; dance around to the right, to the center and back once again, to the center and back twice; dance around to the left, and all dance away.

Try after this a free for all gallop, and then ask who can dance like a Brownie. Tell the children that as Brownies they can cut what capers they like so long as their feet are not in evidence, for Brownies are never heard. Darken the room a little, play very lively but soft music on the upper notes, and the result will be worth seeing, conditions being favorable, which means that the children are as well-behaved and free from ungracious shyness as they should be if they are to go to parties at all.

By this time all are tired and should be invited to seat themselves so that they face an open doorway. Have ready two Brownie dolls to which long threads are attached; pass these threads over the rod which holds the portieres, and, adjusting the threads from a little distance so that the Brownies' feet just touch the floor, pull the strings in time to lively dance music, and you will give the children a treat.

Chapter XI.

WORK AND PLAY.

T seems a great pity in view of childhood's love for pets that they are such nuisances to so many adults. That children should have them, that the fostering of and caring for them has a beneficial effect on character, most parents admit, but the obstacles to having them are usually too great to be surmounted, and only in rare cases is a child indulged to any extent in this regard.

One argument often brought up against the possession of live things is: ''The children tire of them so quickly !'' This ought really to be an argument for, rather than against, such possession. It is child-nature to tire quickly of any toy, plaything or diversion, and even we grown-up people are not absolutely constant in our likes and dislikes. A child is all eagerness for a certain pet. If it is procured for him he delights in it for a time and then begins to neglect it. For this he is usually reproached by the parents who forget how entirely natural it is that one interest should give way to another. This fickleness should make it possible to indulge him in fancies which seem to promise confusion and discomfort to the elders, who look at all such acquisitions as if they were to be permanent. Why not let the child have the rabbit, guinea-pig or pigeon which he wants so much, on condition that he takes care of it, and when the time comes that he ceases to give it the necessary attention pass it on to some other child to whom novelty will give at least a few lessons in devotion.

Boys who have their affairs in their own hands are continually exchanging their possessions, live and otherwise, but little children are being perpetually compelled to conduct their little affairs according to grown-up standards. They are expected because they want a bird, a fish or a lamb always to want it, never to tire of it, and to give it without help or direction the care it needs, whereas if left to themselves they would devote themselves to it for a while and then willingly exchange it for something else, or give it away with pleasure in the giving.

Now and then an attachment between a child and his pet is formed too strong to be easily broken, and when this is the case surely the little one ought to have his dumb friend.

The true inwardness of the whole question of children's deprivations in this regard lies in the fact that their grown-up friends and relatives are not willing to take the necessary trouble, and wherever this is the case of course there is nothing more to be said, except that for their own convenience they deny their children not only a pleasure but a God-given means of development, for a child's passionate love for animals *is* God-given, and given for a purpose.

Not only is a little trouble necessary when pets are kept, but time and space as well. It is too bad that these two latter necessaries do not inevitably accompany a child on his arrival into the family. No place for it—no time for it—it is too much trouble—are familiar words in most children's ears.

But to the mothers who are willing to take the trouble, who have the time, and manufacture the space if need be, let me say a word. Do not, I beg of you, allow your children pets too soon, that is before they are old enough to know how to treat them. Do not give three-year-old a helpless kitten to maul or a dog to tease. Give him a bird or a fish which he cannot handle. If a child is thoughtlessly cruel to such animals as he can handle he can be taught tenderness by having the inaccessible ones substituted, better than by depriving him of all pets and all opportunity for the exercise of the gentler traits of character.

If a child is allowed to have a pet he should be taught how to take care of it, and the daily necessary attention should be as much his responsibility as making beds or dusting is his mother's. If he has to be continually reminded of and nagged into the performance of this duty the pet had better be disposed of and one sought for which may engender such a love in the child as shall make the duty a pleasanter one.

Much has been said and written by kindergartners on the subject of toys, and those commended and recommended which can be really used by the child, such as blocks, crayons, paints, blackboards, stoves, garden tools and the like, all of which is well worthy consideration; but there is a word to be said for toys pure and simple, the tin horses, little wagons, toy animals, miniature houses and stoves and so on. Their value lies in the stimulus or start which they give to a child's imagination. With such a starting point a whole train or sequence of events connects itself, or should do so, in the child's mind, the expression of which forms the play. There are children to whom toys suggest little or nothing, to whom a tin horse is a tin horse and nothing more, and which are by them soon forgotten and discarded. There are others, however, to whom the same toys will be a beginning of a long series of imaginative plays. I once knew three such children, to one of whom was given a tiny milk wagon. At that time a new cable road was the talk of the hour, and one constructed of string, hairpins and spools was in operation across the nursery floor. A long period of happy play was broken by sounds of disagreement and I was finally called for in a tone which told me that something had gone wrong. Several cars were on the track, the little milk wagon in front of them. The owner of the car next to it had " clang-clanged " in vain and I was greeted with " make Mollie get off the track with her milk wagon! I've rang and rang and she won't get off!" Whereupon, seven-year-old Mollie looked up with a placid smile, saying, " I'm a-playing milk wagon. They never get off the track till the car drivers get mad ! "

To these children the merest trifle in the way of a toy suggested any amount of play, and in their ability to *use* the toys so fascinatingly displayed in the shops to round-eyed, wistful-looking children, I find a suggestion of their real purpose. It may be necessary to actually teach some children to play with toys, others may need only a little help, and the normally imaginative ones need no assistance at all, only occasional guidance.

Child psychologists are telling us nowadays that the larger motor activities are the first developed—in other words that the large muscles of the arm and forearm develop before the smaller finger muscles with which fine handwork is done or skilful manipulation accomplished. Kindergartners, believing this to be true, have altered much of their work, and mothers find in the fact a suggestion for the home plays of their babies. I had long noticed that a child under three years old when visiting the kindergarten almost invarially paid but little attention to the blocks, balls and beads on the tables in his absorbed delight in the many red chairs. These he usually proceeded to carry back and forth, to push, to haul, and to place upon the tables, only to take them down again. I know now that when he did this he was joyously seizing an opportunity for developing his larger motor activities, and I would enter here a plea for further opportunities of the same sort for the babies at home.

Most mothers will bear me out in the statement that the playthings which the baby seems to prefer are such as the clothes-basket, the coal-bucket, the wash-boiler and the ice-cream freezer; that is, when he can get these treasures; for usually they are taken away and the little tin horse or red ball substituted in the mistaken idea that these small objects are better suited to his little hands. People think that small toys are what he really wants, that he is mistaken when he thinks he wants the baby-carriage or the foot-tub; but he is not mistaken, he does want these big things, and mothers will do well if as far as possible they will allow their little folks to play with them. If sometimes instead of visiting a toy-shop to buy something to amuse two-year-old they will instead go through the basement of some large department store and buy a bushel-basket or a clothes-line instead of a rubber cat they will be working on the true line of development instead of against it.

I remember watching a baby boy one summer whose choicest plaything was one cylindrical cedar block left in front of the house when the street was paved. With great apparent difficulty, but equal enjoyment, he carried it back and forth, from one place to another, for all sorts of reasons. He sat on it only to rest for further exertions. His wise mother did not object to his playing with it, neither did she insist on carrying it for him. She let nature teach her as well as her little son and both were stronger and wiser for it.

One source of occupation too often overlooked is participation in the routine of housework. The baby always wants to help, and if in spite of the trouble he causes and the extra time his assistance takes he is not only allowed to help, but is actually taught to do so while his mind is open to such teaching, a very efficient little worker will be developed in a few years' time and much real occupation of a pleasurable sort provided. This applies equally to boys and girls, for neither should be deprived of any "something to do" for which the home life affords opportunity. Sympathetic commendation for effort is all that most children need in the way of incentive to work, and the habits thus formed provide for future years.

Real tools, with a little help while the children are learning to use them, should be a part of every home outfit. Instead of the cheap and useless tool-chests sold as toys the real tools purchased as a child grows up to their uses will be found to yield the best results. A very small child can drive tacks into a pine board, and gimlets, augers, saws, hammers and other tools can be used long before it will be safe to put the sharper ones into the little carpenter's hands. Help him to make real things, bird-houses, hurdles, dolls'-sleds, chairs, tables, trellis-sticks and so on. With a very little help and encouragement an active child will soon plan, execute and invent for himself.

Real gardening and real work of all sorts is play to children when they are rightly lead into it. They cannot be expected to do it altogether alone or to keep it up by themselves, but in company with a sympathetic mother who understands how to make real partners of them the amount they accomplish is often surprising.

Fortunate are those children who have an attic in which they can go and play ! Here they find the space they crave and the freedom they love ! Here is a playroom where they can pound nails into the walls and where they need not be afraid of breaking things ! I know one attic where in winter the garden benches are placed, and the hammock and swing put up. Here the children play for hours, in hats and coats if need be, and often with open windows, on days when they cannot go out of doors. I know another attic which has become a gymnasium, where there are turning poles, ropes and rings, punching bags, and best of all, the painter's ladder mentioned in another chapter. The children climb this ladder, walk up it, slide down it, go up hand over hand, weave themselves through it and do with it the thousand other things which would only occur to an active and healthy child.

Manufacturing some sort of a "little house," furnishing it, and living in it, is an occupation which children love, to which they are devoted for weeks which they utterly forget, and to which they fondly return. Indeed, this is true of most of their plays and toys as it is with the pets. Parents often complain that the expensive bicycle, pony-cart, doll-house or tent is used for a while and then neglected. This, let me repeat, is only natural, and the children will return to these treasurers only to discard them and return again. Do not quarrel with nature and she will do her best for you.

She is herself a fine playfellow at all times, but especially in her boisterous moods, and she suits the children excellently when they are in a similar frame of mind. She provides splendid big mud puddles for fortunate barelegged youngsters to splash in!

She sends big winds for children to have fun with, an old umbrella and a wagon or tricycle being part of the play ! She sends warm summer showers to be enjoyed in bathing suits ! She gives ice ponds, snowdrifts, and heaps of leaves to roll in as well as sunshine and flowers and the whole beautiful "Out of Doors!"

LIST OF MATERIALS.

1. Music Books.
2. Story Books.
3. Glass Globe or Aquarium.
4. Garden Box.
5. Blocks.
6. Bean bags.
7. Large Rubber Ball.
8. Colored Paper.
9. Paints.
10. Chalk.
11. Colored Crayons.
12. Blackboard
13. Straws & Parquetry Papers.
14. Hailman Beads.
15. Glass Beads
16. Kindling.
17. Sand.
18. Cedar Blocks.
19. Clay.
20. Weaving Materials.
21. Bristol board cut 8x8
22. Worsted & Worsted Needles.
23. Pricking Needles.
24. Scissors.
25. Gum Tragacanth Paste.
26. Pencils.
27. Drawing Book.
28. Scrap Books for Mounting.
29. Tools.
30. Garden Tools.

Katherine Beebe

Home Occupations for Little Children

ISBN/EAN: 9783337734640

Printed in Europe, USA, Canada, Australia, Japan

Cover: Foto ©Andreas Hilbeck / pixelio.de

More available books at **www.hansebooks.com**